The Signs Were There

NM Aster

Published by NM Aster, 2024.

THE SIGNS WERE THERE

First edition. November 26, 2024.

Copyright © 2024 NM Aster.

ISBN: 979-8230827054

Written by NM Aster.

Also by NM Aster

To My Friend Tshepiso,

This is a result of one of our many questionable discussions!

Introduction

When I stumbled upon these old journals, I wasn't sure what to make of them. They were fragmented, messy, and deeply personal—a chaotic snapshot of a past I'd long tried to forget. Each page held a window into moments I hadn't revisited in years, moments that felt both alien and painfully familiar.

As I sifted through the entries, I saw patterns, connections, and a story taking shape. What you're about to read isn't the full picture—far from it. I've compiled and refined the most relevant parts, leaving the rest buried in the chaos.

These moments, the ones I've chosen to share, tell a story that still haunts me. They're a mosaic of friendships, fears, and fractures in our little world. I hope you'll see why I couldn't let them stay forgotten.

12 February 2023

It's my first time practicing as an independent criminologist. I've spent years preparing for this, listening to my lecturer's words echo in my head: *"Prisoners are just like you and me. They might have acted on their latent malicious desires and gotten incarcerated, but every human being is one decision away from landing themselves in prison."* It always struck me as a necessary truth, a reminder to remain unbiased. But I never felt the need for that lesson. I never carried any self-righteous sense of justice, nor did I ever feel disgusted by the idea of sitting across from a criminal.

What always fascinated me was the idea of peeling back the layers of someone's mind, understanding what pushed them across that invisible line. It felt like a puzzle I was meant to solve, an itch that needed scratching. But as I sit here now, staring at the creased brown file on my desk—the one the district court slapped down like a challenge—I realize how wrong I was.

The moment I saw the name on the first page, I felt the air leave my lungs. *Brandon M.* My pulse quickens, a mix of dread and a sick, electric thrill I can't quite shake. This is the kind of case seasoned professionals would dread handling, a file thick with charges of rape and murder spanning years. And yet, here I am, staring at the details of a life I once knew, trying to reconcile the boy from my past with the monster in the photos.

I glance over the list of charges, each word weighing heavier than the last. **Sexual assault. Homicide. Torture.** The stack of pages seems endless. It's all right here, documented in cold, clinical language, but the reality behind the words is visceral, nauseating. And yet, as I read through the victim testimonies, something darker stirs in me—a fascination I can't deny. I feel it in the pit of my stomach, this unsettling mix of fear, curiosity, and something I'm too ashamed to name. A part of me is almost... excited by the prospect of this interview. The idea that I might finally get to understand him, to dissect his psyche piece by piece.

I remember my first encounter with Brandon back in preschool. Even then, he had a certain magnetism, a charm that made people want to be around him. As the years went by, that allure only grew. By high school, he was the kind of guy everyone wanted to be or be with. But there was always something else lurking beneath the surface, a subtle edge to his laughter, a fleeting darkness in his eyes that most people brushed off. I never did. I noticed it every time. And, if I'm being honest, I was drawn to it, like a moth to a flame.

Maybe I wanted him to notice me. Maybe I wanted to be the one he chose to focus on, even if it meant being pulled into his twisted games. It's a thought that makes my skin crawl now, but I can't deny its existence. I can't lie to myself, not here, not now. As much as I hate to admit it, the idea of Brandon as a predator, as someone who could have easily turned his gaze on me, doesn't fill me with fear alone. There's a sliver of arousal there, a dangerous thrill I can't shake.

I glance up at the clock. Fifteen minutes until I'm supposed to go in. My first real assignment as a criminologist, and it's this. I should feel overwhelmed, anxious about making a good impression. But all I can think about is Brandon, sitting in a cold, sterile room somewhere nearby, waiting for me. It's as if the universe itself orchestrated this meeting, as if every step I took led me back to him.

I slam the file shut, running a hand through my hair. I need to get out of my head. I grab my coat and head for the door, trying to shake the sensation that I'm walking towards something I won't be able to come back from. The hallway feels like a tunnel, the fluorescent lights buzzing overhead like a swarm of angry bees. I reach the interview room and hesitate, my hand hovering over the doorknob. I can feel my heart pounding in my chest, my breath coming in short, shallow bursts.

When I push the door open, he's there. Brandon. He's shackled to the table, but he sits with a casual ease that makes my stomach twist. He looks up as I enter, and for a split second, it's like nothing has changed. It's like we're back in high school, just two guys who might have been friends in another life. Then his lips curl into that familiar smirk, and the illusion shatters.

"Well, well," he drawls, his voice as smooth and mocking as ever. "Look who decided to visit. Long time no see, old friend."

I take a seat across from him, forcing myself to meet his gaze. The room feels smaller than it should, the air thick with a tension I can't quite name. He tilts his head, studying me like I'm the one under the microscope.

"First day on the job, huh?" he says, leaning back as far as his restraints allow. "Didn't think we'd reunite like this."

I swallow hard, trying to keep my voice steady. "Neither did I."

He chuckles, a low, dark sound that sends a shiver down my spine. "Bet you've got a lot of questions. Go on, ask me anything. I'm an open book."

I force a smile, even though I can feel my pulse hammering in my ears. I've got a million questions, but the one that burns brightest, the one that claws at my throat, is one I can't bring myself to voice. *Why do I feel like I'm the one on trial here?*

Instead, I reach for my notebook and pen, flipping to a blank page. I've waited years for this moment, but now that it's here, I'm not sure I'm ready. I'm staring into the eyes of a monster, and all I can think is, *Was it inevitable that we'd end up like this? Him in chains, me across the table, drawn into his orbit once again?*

He leans forward, his smile widening. "Let's get started then. We've got a lot to catch up on, don't we?"

ENTRY #1
25 January 2005

Granny got me a new diary to celebrate my first day of preschool. I'm not sure how she knew I'd like it, but she was right. I've already wasted the first few pages with my attempts at drawing Ash Ketchum and a very unrecognizable Pikachu. There's also a Goku with hair that's way too spiky and a Vegeta whose face looks more like a squashed potato. But still, I'm proud of them—those scribbles feel like little victories.

I've watched enough all-American family movies to know what people use diaries for. They're supposed to be secret books where you spill your thoughts and dreams, or talk about crushes (yuck). I don't think I'll be writing about that anytime soon, but I do want to record all the new friends I'm going to make today. It's the first day of preschool, after all! And who knows, maybe I'll have lots of stories to tell by the end of it.

I'm especially excited to see Mrs. Karen again. She's the teacher who interviewed Granny and me just a few days ago. I liked her right away. She seemed really kind, and she had this soft, patient smile that made me feel like everything was going to be okay. I remember her kneeling down to my level and asking about my favorite games and shows, as if what I had to say really mattered. It made me feel seen, like I wasn't just a kid she had to deal with but someone worth listening to.

There's a weird kind of flutter in my stomach right now—part excitement, part nervousness. I've never really spent a whole day away from Granny before. It's just been the two of us for as long as I can remember, and even though she says I'm ready for this, I can't help but wonder if she'll miss me as much as I'll miss her.

But maybe I'll meet someone today who likes Pokémon too. Someone who'll know exactly why I keep drawing Pikachu with those zigzag cheeks. I guess I'll find out soon enough.

For now, I'm closing this diary and putting on my new Spider-Man backpack. Granny says it's good luck to start something new with a smile, so I'm going to try that. Here goes nothing.

ENTRY #2
26 January 2005

Today was fun. My first day of preschool, and I already made a friend. I think his name was Brendon, or maybe it was Brandon? Honestly, after everything that happened today, I completely forgot what he said his name was. He was just so much fun to hang out with. I was a little nervous at first, but the day flew by faster than I expected.

We were assigned to the same classroom, which was cool. I really thought Mrs. Karen was going to be my teacher, but instead, I got Ms. Bubbles. I'm not sure that's even her real name, but that's what we all call her. She's this chubby, middle-aged woman with a smile so fake that it kind of makes my skin crawl. It's like she's just here to collect a paycheck, not really caring about the kids or how we feel. I'm always good at spotting that stuff, even the tiny things—people's little tells that they think no one notices. I got it from my parents, I guess. They still think I believe in the tooth fairy, but I stopped believing a long time ago.

In fact, last month, I caught Granny sneaking into my room late at night. She thought I was asleep, but I wasn't. She slid her hand under my pillow, thinking she was still playing the game. I just laid there, pretending to sleep while she slipped a twenty-dollar bill under my pillow. I didn't say anything.

What's the point? It's not like I'm going to ruin the fun for her. I got twenty bucks out of it, and Granny thinks she's still fooling me.

But anyway, back to Brendon/Brandon. He's a funny guy. He almost got me into trouble on the first day, though. I'm still not sure if he knew it was wrong, but he tried to convince me to join him in something called "panty-watching." He kept trying to look under Lisa's skirt—she's one of our classmates, and her dad's some rich car dealer. She's always got the nicest clothes, and today she was wearing these lime-green underwear that Brandon thought were hilarious.

I didn't get why it was funny. Honestly, I just didn't understand what the big deal was about seeing someone's underwear. But Brendon/Brandon? He was practically in stitches over it. I didn't want to be a party pooper, so I didn't say anything, but part of me felt kind of weird about it. Like, I wasn't sure if I was doing the right thing by just going along with it.

Even though he's a little... strange, I think he's still a cool guy. He's got that thing about him, you know? That energy that makes people follow him. But when he tells me what to do, he gets this look in his eyes, like he's daring me to say no. And I don't know why, but that part of him scares me a little. It's not like he ever hits anyone or anything, but the way he can make me feel like I have to do what he says—like I don't have a choice—it's a weird feeling.

But I'll keep hanging out with him, I think. He's interesting, and, well, I guess I want to see what else he gets up to. Maybe he's just a little too much sometimes, but that's okay, right? He's fun, and I can always try to be careful. At least, I think I can.

ENTRY #3
24 September 2005

Today was Brandon's birthday. His dad came to school and brought a gigantic themed cake for the whole class to share. It was one of those big, multi-tiered ones you only see in movies, decorated with bright, colorful icing. Everyone was excited, but I couldn't stop looking at Brandon's dad. His arms were covered in scary-looking tattoos that stretched down his bulky forearms, and every time he handed out a slice of cake, he gave Brandon this quick, cold glare that made the air freeze for a second. It wasn't the first time I'd seen him look at Brandon like that, but it made me feel uneasy every time. It seemed like Brandon had done something to make his dad angry, though I wasn't sure what.

Brandon wasn't his usual self today. He was jittery, tense, like a rubber band stretched too tight. He hardly spoke to anyone, just poking at his cake or staring off into the distance. It was like he was on edge the whole time, and I could tell it wasn't just because of the party. Whatever happened between him and his dad this morning had shaken him up. But I didn't want to ask. I didn't want to get involved in whatever it was.

He's always been in trouble, and I've noticed the way Ms. Bubbles doesn't seem to like him much. I overheard her and Mrs. Karen talking in the halls during recess yesterday, their voices low and hushed. They mentioned something about 'abuse,' and though I couldn't hear all of it, my gut told me it was serious. The way they whispered made my skin crawl. I tried to listen in, but Ms. Bubbles spotted me and gave me this sharp look, like she knew what I was doing. She didn't even have to say anything. I could tell from the way she looked at me that I was being naughty.

I didn't want to get into trouble, so I quickly walked away. Granny always told me that eavesdropping was for naughty boys, and I didn't want her calling Granny on me. I didn't want to be punished at home—Granny's wooden spoon is no joke.

Later, during playtime, I saw Brandon again. He was trying to look under the skirts of some girls from the other classes, his eyes darting around like he was trying to be sneaky. My stomach sank. I didn't want him to get into more trouble with Ms. Bubbles, so I went over and gently told him to stop. I tried to be nice about it, like how Granny would talk to me when I wasn't being good, but he just ignored me and kept doing it. It wasn't the first time. He'd been warned so many times since we started school. The teachers had said something to him at least ten times already, but he kept pushing the boundaries.

Then it happened. He slapped me. Hard. I couldn't believe it at first. The sting on my cheek was still sharp, and I felt my face heat up with embarrassment. I wanted to cry, to shout at him, but I couldn't. I didn't want to get him into more trouble, not with the way he was already acting, not with how his dad looked at him earlier. The last thing I wanted was for him to get punished again. I didn't know what would happen if someone told on him, but I was scared.

So instead, I held my tears in. I forced an apology out of him, which he reluctantly gave. He mumbled it like he didn't even mean it, but I guess it was something. He was always trying to look tough, like he didn't care about anything, but I could see it in his eyes.

His hazel brown eyes were so full of pain—like he was holding in a sea of tears, all swirling behind those dark, heavy lids. It was like he was trapped inside something, like he was trying to push it all down but couldn't. I didn't know what it was, but I could feel it.

Brandon's always been cool in a way, like he's got this mysterious, dangerous thing about him. But now, I'm starting to wonder if maybe it's not so cool after all.

ENTRY #4
12 October 2005

Today was another one of those days. The ones where everything feels heavy, like something's wrong but you can't quite put your finger on it. It was Brandon.

He came to preschool without a lunchbox again today. It's become a pattern by now, something I've stopped thinking too much about because, well, it's not like it's a big deal, right? But it was the way he didn't even seem to care about it, his eyes hollow, his hands buried deep in his pockets like he was trying to hide from everyone. His clothes were worse than usual, too. The sleeves of his shirt were torn at the cuffs, like he'd been yanking at them absentmindedly. His pants were frayed around the edges, the kind of damage you get from wearing them too often. And yet, there was something about it that made me feel uneasy. Maybe it was because, for the first time, I actually noticed the dirt under his nails, the way his shoes seemed to be falling apart, or the fact that his hair was messier than usual, as if he hadn't bothered to comb it in days.

He didn't look like the same Brandon I'd met at the beginning of the year. Back then, he was loud, a bit mischievous, always the center of attention. He had a way of getting under people's skin, pushing the boundaries and seeing how far he could go before someone would stop him. It was fun back then, a little rebellious in the way kids that age are supposed to be. But today, Brandon didn't seem to care about anything. He shuffled into the classroom without even greeting anyone, his gaze fixed on the floor as he slid into his seat like he was trying to disappear into it.

It wasn't just his lack of lunch that bothered me, though. It was the smell. The stale scent of cigarettes clung to him like a second skin, so strong it nearly made me gag when he walked past me on his way to his seat. It was a smell that didn't belong on a child, a smell that made me think of late nights, angry voices, and things I didn't want to imagine. I'd noticed it before, but it was worse today, like he'd been around it for hours.

I don't know why I noticed it so much today. Maybe it was because I was starting to pay more attention. I wasn't the only one who noticed the bruises, though. They were harder to ignore now that they were showing more often. Today, as he moved to sit at his desk, I saw the purple bruise on his arm, just above his wrist. It was the same color as the one I'd seen last week, and the one the week before that. I couldn't help but wonder where they were coming from, who was making them.

Brandon never talked about his dad. I didn't know what happened when he went home, but I knew enough to guess. I'd seen his dad a few times. He was the kind of guy who walked into a room and immediately made everyone feel tense, like you had to stand a little straighter and watch your words. He was tall, with a neck like a tree trunk and muscles that bulged even under his old, faded t-shirt. His arms were covered in tattoos that made him look even more intimidating, and his face was always set in a frown. He didn't look at Brandon the way a dad should look at his son. He looked at him like he was a nuisance, someone who needed to be dealt with and put in his place. It wasn't a look I could ignore. I could see the way Brandon's shoulders slumped whenever his dad came to school to drop him off or pick him up. It was like he was trying to make himself as small as possible, hoping to avoid the glare of those cold eyes.

Today, it seemed like the bruise on Brandon's arm was just another reminder of what was happening at home. I didn't know the whole story, but I could guess enough. And it made me feel sick. I wanted to ask him what happened, to tell him he didn't deserve it, but I didn't know how. I was scared that he would shut me out, or worse, that he'd lash out at me the way he did with Ms. Bubbles earlier.

It wasn't just the bruises that had changed. It was the way he was acting, too. He was more aggressive now. He wasn't the same funny, reckless kid I used to think he was. Now, he was quick to anger, snapping at anyone who got too close, including me. During playtime, when I was sitting on the swings, he came over and pushed me hard enough that I nearly lost my balance and fell off. I don't know why he did it, or maybe I do, but it didn't make it any easier to deal with. I couldn't understand it. It wasn't like him to act like that, but every time I saw him now, there was this look in his eyes—this anger, this hurt—that made me feel like he was a completely different person.

Ms. Bubbles didn't help things. She seemed to avoid him now, like she couldn't figure out how to deal with him. Every time she asked him to do something, he would glare at her like she was the one who had done something wrong. He wasn't even trying to hide it anymore. He was loud, demanding, and rude, and it was like no one knew what to do about it.

By the time lunch came around, the tension was thick in the air. No one said anything out loud, but we all knew that something wasn't right with Brandon. He was different, and we were all starting to notice it. It was only when Ms. Bubbles tried to get him to sit down at the lunch table that the first real confrontation of the day happened.

"Brandon," she said, her voice unsteady, "please sit down and eat your lunch."

Brandon didn't even look at her. Instead, he stared straight ahead, his face expressionless. "I'm not hungry," he muttered, his voice low and rough.

"But you didn't even bring a lunch," Ms. Bubbles pressed. "We can't have you skipping lunch again."

"I'm fine," he snapped, his words sharp, cutting through the air like a slap. His eyes met hers then, cold and defiant. "Just leave me alone."

That was when the room fell silent. Everyone knew something was wrong, but no one knew what to say. The tension was so thick you could almost feel it in the air, like something was about to break. I glanced at Mrs. Karen, who was watching from the doorway, her face pale. She seemed to be waiting for something to happen, but I wasn't sure what.

Later in the day, after everyone had gone home, Ms. Bubbles gathered us all together and announced that a school meeting had been scheduled for the following day. All of our parents were to attend, supposedly because of Brandon's behavior.

I didn't know what to think about that. I didn't know what they were going to say, or what they were going to do. But I knew it was serious. Mrs. Karen had mentioned something about how much trouble Brandon had been causing, and I could see the worry in her eyes when she spoke. She was clearly concerned about him, but there was something else there too. Something I couldn't put my finger on.

The rest of the day went by in a blur. I tried not to think about the meeting, about what would happen to Brandon, but it was hard. It was impossible to ignore the way his world seemed to be falling apart around him. His dad didn't seem to care. Ms. Bubbles didn't seem to know what to do. And I... I didn't know what to do either.

Maybe, deep down, I was just as scared of him as everyone else. Maybe I was scared of what he was becoming. Or maybe I was just scared of what would happen if he didn't change.

I don't know what will happen at that meeting tomorrow, but I can't shake the feeling that it's only the beginning. And whatever happens, I'm not sure I'm ready for it.

ENTRY #5
24 October 2005

It's strange how fast everything can change, how one moment everything seems familiar, like it always will be, and then—just like that—it's gone.

Brandon hasn't been back to school since that meeting. It's been over two weeks now, and I can't help but feel like something is wrong. When I ask about him, I get nothing but vague responses, a tight-lipped silence from Ms. Bubbles, Mrs. Karen, and even my Gran. I can tell they're hiding something, but no one will tell me what. Every time I ask where he is, the answers are deflected with a simple, "Oh, he's not feeling well," or "He's taking some time off." But it doesn't make sense. He never said goodbye. He didn't even pack his things or leave a note. It's like he vanished.

I'm not sure when it started, but somewhere in the past few days, it hit me: I miss him. I never thought I'd feel this way, never thought I'd even admit it, but I do. His absence is like a weight, sitting heavily on my chest. It's like someone removed the color from everything around me, and all that's left is a dull, lifeless world. Without him, school is quieter, less interesting, and, honestly, more lonely.

At first, I didn't know how to process it. I'd find myself looking around, expecting to see him standing there, causing some kind of trouble or telling me to follow him to some new mischief. But he's not there. The playground is quieter without his loud laugh or his daredevil antics. Even Ms. Bubbles seems like she's trying to avoid looking at me, as if she's afraid I'll ask the wrong questions again.

Gran, too. She's been weird about it, too. I thought she would have told me what happened, but she hasn't. She doesn't even bring it up, which is unusual for her. She's always been open, always willing to talk about things. But now, when I try to ask, she just brushes it off, telling me to stop worrying about things I don't need to know. "There's nothing to worry about, dear," she says, always with a smile that doesn't quite reach her eyes. It's like she's trying to convince herself more than me.

I can't shake the feeling that something's happened to Brandon, something worse than what I already know. I'm not stupid—I can put the pieces together. His dad, the bruises, the cigarette smell, the anger—it was all a sign of something bigger, something ugly. And now he's gone, just disappeared. I don't know if I should be relieved or terrified. Maybe both.

Gran told me I had to stop focusing on Brandon, that I needed to make new friends. She says it like it's so simple, like just snapping my fingers and suddenly I'll be surrounded by people who care about me. But it's not like that, is it? You don't just replace someone like that. Brandon might have been a mess, but he was mine, in a way. He was the only person who seemed to get me, even if we didn't always get along. It's not easy to let go of someone like that.

So, I've been trying. I've been trying to make new friends. But it's harder than I thought. The other kids don't seem to get me the way Brandon did. They're fine, I guess, but there's this wall between us, something I can't seem to break down. It's like they're all speaking a different language, and no matter how much I try to talk, I can't get them to understand.

There's a boy named Michael who sits next to me in class now. He's always asking me if I want to play football, but I don't really like football. It's not that I don't want to be friends with him, it's just... I don't know. It's not the same. It's not like it was with Brandon. It feels forced. But I go along with it because that's what you're supposed to do, right? You're supposed to make new friends when the old ones disappear.

And then there's Rachel. She's in my art class, and she's always sketching in her notebook, drawing weird creatures and strange landscapes. She talks a lot, but I can't help but think she's just talking to fill the silence. She's nice, but she's not *Brandon*. She doesn't have that way of making everything feel... real, you know? Like when Brandon was around, things felt raw and honest. With her, everything feels like a performance, like she's pretending to be something she's not.

Sometimes I catch myself looking at the empty space next to me, expecting to see Brandon sitting there. But he's not. And I don't know what to do about it. It's like a hole inside of me that no one else can fill. Every time I try to push it down, to make myself forget, it just grows bigger.

I wonder where he is. I wonder if he's okay. I wonder if he misses me, or if he's forgotten about me completely. Part of me hopes he's somewhere safe, away from whatever it was that was hurting him. But another part of me is terrified that he's not, that he's somewhere worse, stuck in a world that doesn't care about him. I can't stop thinking about him, and it drives me crazy.

I try to talk about it with Gran, but she just tells me I need to focus on my own life, that Brandon's not coming back, and I should stop worrying about him. But how can I stop worrying about him when I don't even know what happened to him? How can I stop when everything around me feels... off?

So, I've been trying to keep busy. I'm trying to focus on school, to make the best of it, but it's hard. Every time I look at the empty desk in the corner of the room, I remember Brandon's half-sarcastic smile and his too-loud laugh. I remember the way he used to say things like, "You're too soft, man," when he thought I was being too nice.

I don't know if I'll ever get over this. I don't know if I'm supposed to. But it feels like a part of me is missing now that he's gone. I think I need to know what happened to him, even if no one else will tell me. Maybe once I know, I'll be able to let go. But until then, I'll just keep wondering.

I miss you, Brandon. I miss you more than I thought I would.

ENTRY #6
12 January 2006

I never thought I would see him again.

After Brandon disappeared from our old school, I was told little to nothing. Mrs. Edwards, our new first-grade teacher, had come with some story about family matters, something vague about him having to take time off, and none of the other kids knew anything more than I did. But there were whispers. I could see it in the way the other kids looked at me when I asked about him, as if they already knew something I didn't.

But here he was, standing in the doorway of our new classroom like a ghost who'd just returned from the dead. It wasn't like he'd been gone for just a few months. It felt like years had passed.

Brandon's eyes were darker now, a little older, but still the same—the same unsettling, distant look that would send a shiver down your spine if you looked too long. His clothes were tattered, far worse than the scruffy jeans and worn-out sneakers I remembered. They looked like they'd been through hell. His face was pale, a little thinner than I remembered, and his hair was messier.

But what stood out most was the way he held himself. He wasn't like the rest of us. He had an air of defiance, as though he were just barely tolerating this whole "school" thing. I could tell right away that nothing about his absence had been as simple as Mrs. Edwards had led us to believe. It was more than just "family matters" or a few weeks off for some sort of trivial reason. Something darker lingered in the space between us.

That day, after he returned, I found myself watching him more than I should've, eyes following him like a shadow, trying to see what had changed.

He was different. And it scared me.

Mrs. Edwards, with her sharp features and severe tone, had already given us our first lesson on the importance of behaving in class. "You're not babies anymore," she'd told us, her stern eyes sweeping across the group, "so act like first graders." She was the kind of teacher who expected to be respected, and she made it clear from the start that she didn't tolerate nonsense. But when Brandon walked in, her face shifted ever so slightly—just enough for me to catch the flash of hesitation.

I couldn't help but notice how she avoided looking directly at him when he took his seat near the back of the class. It wasn't the same reaction I'd seen from her when the rest of us entered.

The day went by as usual—there were new faces, some familiar from kindergarten, and the typical first-grade activities. But every now and then, I'd catch Brandon's gaze, and it was like something in the air changed. He wasn't saying much, but he didn't need to. His eyes did all the talking. They were full of quiet resentment, a darkness I couldn't fully grasp at that age. It was unnerving, and yet... I found myself drawn to it.

During recess, things started to show cracks. I was playing with a few of the other kids when I noticed Brandon off by himself, leaning against the swing set, watching some of the girls playing jump rope.

I tried to ignore it, but I couldn't.

He wasn't just looking at them—he was watching them. More specifically, he was watching their skirts.

At first, I didn't understand. Why was he staring so intently, like he was studying them? My thoughts ran in circles as I tried to make sense of it, but before I could act, Mrs. Edwards was there, calling for all of us to line up.

But it wasn't the first time.

ENTRY #7

13 January 2006

Today during our art period, Brandon's behavior escalated. I could feel the tension building in the classroom, but no one dared speak up. I think we all understood, even at that age, that something was off with him. We weren't supposed to question it. We were just kids, and kids don't question things like that.

But I couldn't help myself. I watched him closely as he picked at the edges of his drawing, tapping his pencil on the desk in agitation. He seemed out of place—like he was wearing a mask he didn't want anyone to see through.

I decided to approach him during break, just to talk. Maybe, just maybe, if I tried to reconnect, things would be like they used to be—normal.

"Hey, Brandon," I said hesitantly, sitting down beside him. He didn't look at me at first, just continued fiddling with his pencil.

"What's up?" I tried again, hoping for some kind of response.

"Nothing," he muttered, his voice low. But then his eyes flicked to mine, and there was something in them—something almost predatory. A flicker of recognition, like he remembered me, but it was tainted by something darker. It wasn't the friendly glance I remembered from the past.

For the first time, I felt the hairs on the back of my neck stand up.

Mrs. Edwards caught the change in the air too. By the end of the week, she had called a special meeting with the parents of the class. She made it clear that Brandon's behavior was becoming an issue, but she refused to name it outright. She skirted around the subject with vague statements about "adjusting" to the new environment and "being sensitive" to his past.

I overheard a snippet of conversation between Mrs. Edwards and Mr. Collins one day, though, as I lingered by the door.

"There's something more to him," Mrs. Edwards had whispered. "He's... not right. I'm concerned."

It made my stomach twist. What did she mean by that? I hadn't heard her talk about any other student like that before. It was unsettling, and it made me wonder—was it just me, or was there something really wrong with Brandon?

The school meeting that followed was tense. My Gran came with me, and the teacher made an effort to sugarcoat things. But it was clear there was something they weren't telling us. My Gran was furious by the end, a mix of confusion and anger clouding her features.

"That boy," she muttered under her breath as we walked out, "There's something wrong with him, and I don't think anyone's doing enough about it."

I couldn't help but feel a pang of guilt. Brandon had become a project in my mind—a mystery I had to solve. There was this feeling, deep down, that maybe if I understood him better, if I spent more time with him, I could somehow fix things. But I didn't know how. I didn't even know where to start.

ENTRY #8

18 January 2006

This week, things got worse. Much worse. Brandon had gotten into a fight with one of the other kids—something about a disagreement over a game they were playing. When the teacher intervened, he lashed out at her, shoving her hand away and calling her a name I didn't quite catch. It was something angry, something bitter, and it sent a chill through the room.

Afterward, Brandon spent the rest of the day sulking in the corner, barely participating in class activities. But as much as I wanted to feel sorry for him, I couldn't shake the fear growing in the pit of my stomach. It wasn't just the fact that he had been violent. It was how easily he did it, how unbothered he seemed by the consequences of his actions.

I had seen a lot of kids act out, sure. But not like this. Not with that same coldness.

By the end of the week, I had almost come to the conclusion that maybe Brandon wasn't the same person I once thought he was. His presence didn't excite me anymore. It scared me. And I didn't know what to do about it.

I kept my distance. But I couldn't forget him.

Even though I was afraid of what Brandon was becoming, a part of me still longed for the closeness we once had. It was the strangest feeling, like being trapped between loyalty and terror.

There was no going back now. Whatever Brandon had become, I was helpless to stop it.

Entry #9
12 November 2009

It's almost the end of our elementary school journey. The teachers keep droning on about how middle school is a battlefield we'll never survive if we don't start taking things seriously. No one seems too concerned. After years of hearing the same recycled warnings, we've grown immune to their idle threats.

Conversations among my classmates now center around which middle school they'll be attending. It's a bittersweet time. There's excitement for what's ahead, but an unspoken sadness lingers—it's the realization that this might be the last time we see some of our friends.

Brandon and I? We've drifted apart. These days, we're on a polite "hello-hi" basis. He's been spending most of his time with Todd, a wiry, sharp-tongued boy who shares Brandon's flair for rebellion. Todd transferred to our school last year and immediately made his mark with a knack for goading others into petty mischief. Together, he and Brandon are the kind of duo that keeps teachers on edge but stops just shy of crossing lines that lead to serious trouble.

I can't say I've been sad about the distance between us. Our interactions had always carried an unspoken tension I couldn't quite place, a mix of awe and discomfort that left me uneasy.

Still, there's a pang of nostalgia when I think back to preschool when we were inseparable—back when I thought I'd found a lifelong friend.

Suzy, my seatmate, shared a piece of her apple crumble with me today. Her mom bakes like a dream; every bite was a perfect balance of crisp tartness and buttery sweetness. Suzy and I have bonded over our mutual love of books and our amateur attempts to dissect political discussions overheard at dinner tables. She's one of the smartest people I know, someone whose thoughts challenge me to think differently.

But Suzy's leaving. She'll be moving to the city for middle school, where she'll undoubtedly thrive. It feels unfair, though. First Brandon, now Suzy—it seems like everyone who's meant something to me is slipping away.

At recess, I saw Brandon and Todd huddled behind the bike shed, their heads bent conspiratorially. Brandon's been different lately. His unruliness, once sporadic, seems more calculated now. His behavior isn't just mischief—it's sharper, like there's something bubbling underneath the surface.

"Hey!" Todd's voice broke into my thoughts. He must've spotted me watching. "What are you staring at, loser?"

I quickly turned away, pretending to be absorbed in a game of tag some younger kids were playing nearby. From the corner of my eye, I saw Brandon smirk. Not the mischievous smirk I remembered from preschool, but something colder, almost mocking. It struck me then that I didn't know him anymore—not really.

Back in class, Ms. Trelawney was giving one of her infamous lectures. She's our homeroom teacher, a no-nonsense woman with a booming voice that commands attention. Today, her target was homework—or the lack thereof.

"You think middle school will tolerate this?" she barked, waving a stack of incomplete assignments. "You're in for a rude awakening!"

Brandon leaned back in his chair, arms crossed, with a look of bored defiance. Todd, seated next to him, muttered something under his breath that made Brandon snicker. Suzy shot them both a disapproving look.

"Brandon!" Ms. Trelawney's voice snapped like a whip. "Care to share what's so funny with the rest of the class?"

"No, ma'am," Brandon replied, his tone dripping with mock innocence.

"Then sit up straight and pay attention," she said sternly, though the weariness in her voice suggested she'd long given up on him.

After school, I lingered at the gates, waiting for Granny to pick me up. Suzy was there too, clutching her notebook and chatting with a group of girls. Brandon and Todd walked past us, their conversation punctuated by laughter. Brandon glanced my way, and for a brief moment, our eyes met. There was no smile, no acknowledgment—just a fleeting look that left me wondering what he was thinking.

"Hey," Suzy said, pulling me from my thoughts. "Are you okay?"

"Yeah," I replied, though I wasn't sure it was true.

Granny's car pulled up, and I climbed in, waving goodbye to Suzy. As we drove home, I couldn't shake the feeling that something was changing. The friends I'd relied on, the dynamics I'd grown used to—all of it felt like sand slipping through my fingers.

That night, I lay in bed, staring at the glow-in-the-dark stars on my ceiling. The day's events replayed in my mind, a jumble of faces and voices. Brandon's smirk, Suzy's laughter, Ms. Trelawney's frustration—it all swirled together in a confusing mess of emotions.

I missed the Brandon I used to know, the boy who'd been my first friend. I missed Suzy, even though she hadn't left yet. Most of all, I missed the simplicity of our early school days when everything felt lighter, less complicated.

Tomorrow's another day, I thought, but the sentiment rang hollow. For the first time, I felt the weight of growing up—the inevitability of change and the bittersweet realization that nothing stays the same.

Entry #10
13 April 2010

A few months into middle school, and it already feels like a bad fit. I could sense the shift from day one—the hallways are louder, the cliques tighter, and the atmosphere far less forgiving. Most of the friendly faces I knew scattered to other schools, leaving me to navigate this new world with strangers. What's worse, middle school brought with it a flood of crass, unruly kids from other elementary schools. Their presence turned the environment from uncomfortable to outright hostile.

Of course, some constants remained. Brandon, my dear old friend, is here, still glued to Todd's side. Those two are practically inseparable now—a modern-day Siamese twin act, with a bond so tight it overshadows anything we ever had back in preschool. I don't know if I'd call it admiration or jealousy, but seeing them together stings in ways I can't fully understand. They do everything as a unit—class projects, lunch, gym class. Their camaraderie is effortless, like two pieces of a puzzle locking into place.

What I don't envy, though, is their nickname: *"the gay couple."*

The name started as a joke, one of those childish ways kids try to get under each other's skin. Nobody really believes it, of course. It's just their way of poking fun at how close Brandon and Todd are. But the name stuck, whispered in hallways, shouted across the soccer field. I doubt they care; they've built a fortress around themselves, shrugging off insults with the kind of confidence I've never had.

My experience has been different.

I admit it—I've always been a bit on the feminine side. Growing up so closely attached to Gran and Suzy shaped me in ways I can't ignore. I prefer books to soccer, quiet to chaos. And here, that's enough to paint a target on my back. The teasing started small: a snicker here, a sarcastic comment there. But it didn't take long for the bullies to escalate.

Now, I'm "Madam."

The name is spat at me in class, whispered behind my back, and, worst of all, echoed by the very teachers meant to protect me. I don't think they realize the damage they're doing, or maybe they don't care. Either way, the humiliation sinks deeper every time I hear it.

The World Cup is a few months away, and you'd think it was Christmas with how much the school is hyping it up. Soccer fever has gripped the boys in my grade. Every spare minute is spent kicking a ball around, strategizing for imaginary matches, or arguing over who's the greatest player of all time. Mr. Clynes, the gym teacher, has made it his personal mission to turn us all into mini-athletes.

I, however, am no soccer fan.

Gym class has become a battleground. In the changing room, the teasing turns crueler. They mock my slender frame, my uncoordinated attempts at kicking a ball. I'm shoved, my gym clothes go missing, and once, someone "accidentally" dumped an entire water bottle on my head. The humiliation piles on until I dread every Tuesday and Thursday when gym is scheduled.

Brandon and Todd aren't involved in the bullying. At least, not directly. But their silence feels just as painful. I've caught Brandon watching me once or twice when the teasing gets particularly bad. His expression is unreadable—neither sympathy nor malice, just a blank stare. I want to believe that somewhere deep down, the boy I knew still cares. But then he'll turn back to Todd, and they'll share a laugh, and I'm reminded just how far we've drifted.

Lunch is my only sanctuary. I've found a quiet spot in the far corner of the schoolyard, behind the art building, where I can eat in peace. There's an old bench there, half-hidden by overgrown bushes, and it's become my refuge. I spend my lunch breaks with a book in one hand and a sandwich in the other, letting the stories carry me far away from this reality.

Today, though, my solitude was interrupted.

"Hey, you okay?"

I looked up to see Eliza, one of the quieter girls in my class. She's never spoken to me before, but there's a kindness in her eyes that makes me want to trust her.

"Yeah," I lied, closing my book.

"You're always over here by yourself," she said, sitting down beside me. "I thought maybe you could use some company."

We talked for the rest of lunch. About books, mostly—she loves fantasy novels, just like me. For the first time in weeks, I felt a flicker of hope. Maybe middle school wouldn't be so bad after all.

The day ended on a sour note.

As I was leaving school, Brandon and Todd walked past me, laughing about something I didn't catch. I called out to Brandon—just his name, a simple greeting—but he didn't even glance my way.

Todd noticed, though.

"Still trying, huh?" he sneered, loud enough for others to hear. "Move on, Madam. He doesn't care."

The laughter that followed burned hotter than any insult.

I walked home in silence, my shoulders heavy with the weight of the day. Middle school isn't what I hoped it would be. It's lonelier, harsher. The world feels bigger, and yet I've never felt smaller.

But as I sat at my desk that evening, staring at a blank page in my diary, I thought about Eliza. About the quiet kindness she offered me when I needed it most. Maybe not all hope is lost.

For now, I'll take it one day at a time.

ENTRY #11
15 September 2010

Today will haunt me for a long time.

The morning began with little fanfare, but by third period, whispers spread like wildfire: Brandon and Todd had been called into the principal's office. The rumor was that they'd been caught harassing girls—again. It wasn't the first time, and it probably wouldn't be the last. The two of them operated like a pack of wild dogs, untamed and unpredictable, constantly pushing boundaries.

I tried to dismiss it. After all, Brandon had long since ceased to matter to me—or so I told myself. But during recess, I found myself passing by the boys' restroom, drawn by strange noises that didn't belong. Laughter, muffled and conspiratorial, mixed with the faint sound of something else—something I couldn't quite place.

Curiosity got the better of me, and before I knew it, I was stepping inside.

There they were, huddled at one of the sinks like two wolves plotting their next move. Todd noticed me first, his expression shifting into a sly grin. "Hey, come here!" he called, motioning for me to join them.

I hesitated, standing frozen in the doorway. Brandon looked up, his smirk widening when he saw me. "Yeah, come on," he echoed, his tone smooth and coaxing.

Against my better judgment, I approached.

"Check this out," Todd said, shoving a phone toward me.

The screen lit up with images I wasn't prepared for—pornography. Explicit, raw, and unfiltered. Men and women tangled in acts I didn't even know existed, their bodies moving in ways that made my cheeks burn and my stomach flip.

My first instinct was to look away, but my eyes betrayed me, lingering on the screen longer than they should have. I was torn between the instinct to flee and a strange, magnetic pull to stay.

Brandon was watching me, his gaze sharp and predatory. "So," he said, his voice dropping into a low, teasing drawl. "What do you think? Huh? How does it make you feel... down there?"

My heart raced as he took a step closer, the space between us disappearing in an instant. His face was uncomfortably close to mine, his breath warm and heavy against my skin. His eyes flicked down briefly, then back up, as if daring me to answer.

"How does it feel?" he whispered, his lips so close to mine that for a terrifying moment, I thought he might kiss me.

I couldn't speak. My throat felt tight, my palms clammy. Then it happened: the telltale stirring, an unwelcome reaction to the images on the screen and the charged proximity of Brandon. My body betrayed me in the worst way possible.

My hands shot down to cover myself, but it was too late. They saw.

Brandon's grin turned wicked, his eyes lighting up with triumph. He stepped back, laughing—a deep, mocking sound that echoed off the tiled walls.

"He's hard!" he said, nudging Todd, who immediately burst into laughter, doubling over with the force of it.

"Holy shit," Todd gasped, barely able to catch his breath. "Brandon, you've got him going!"

And then, the words that sealed my humiliation:

"He really is gay," Brandon said, his voice dripping with smug satisfaction.

Todd laughed even harder, slapping Brandon on the back. "Way to go, man. You proved it!"

Their laughter filled the room, loud and merciless. I stood there, frozen, my face burning with a mix of shame, anger, and something else I couldn't name.

"Come on, don't be mad," Brandon said, his tone mockingly conciliatory. "We're just messing with you."

But I wasn't just mad—I was furious. Furious at them, at myself, at this entire situation. I wanted to scream, to cry, to hit something. Instead, I turned and fled, their laughter following me out the door and into the hallway.

The rest of the day passed in a blur. I avoided Brandon and Todd like the plague, ducking into classrooms and taking the long way around to avoid any chance of running into them. But no matter where I went, I couldn't escape the memory of Brandon's breath on my skin, his words ringing in my ears.

"He really is gay."

It wasn't just a taunt. It was a weapon, sharp and precise, aimed straight at my insecurities. And the worst part? A small, hidden part of me wondered if he was right.

I hated him for what he did, but more than that, I hated the way he made me feel. Any form of care I had for him died in that bathroom.

ENTRY #12
23 September 2010

About a week or so has passed since the bathroom incident, and my school life has become a total nightmare. Those two a**holes had already spread the rumor around the entire school. Kids from other classes, who'd up until that point never even spoken to me, suddenly felt bold enough to tease me for being gay—or at least, that's what they said. They didn't use the exact word "gay." No, they used a much meaner one—a slur I had never even heard before. It wasn't until I went home that night and timidly Googled it that I fully understood its weight. The word burned on the screen, searing itself into my memory as if branded there.

The rumor spread like wildfire, faster than I could have imagined. Even the girls joined in. It wasn't the overt teasing of the boys, though, that got to me. Something about the way the girls smirked as they whispered stung more. A group of them, self-proclaimed fashionistas who ruled the hallway near the lockers, had started a game of leaving bright pink underwear on my desk during lunch breaks. "What color are you wearing today?" one of them, Lily, had asked mockingly, the others doubling over with laughter. I wanted to yell, to scream, to do anything to shut them up—but I couldn't. Their cruelty felt sharper, more cutting. It made me question everything. If this was what it meant to "like" girls, to exist in their world, then maybe I was better off being what they accused me of.

Recess became a minefield. Brandon and Todd loomed on the edges of the schoolyard, surrounded by their posse of boys. From a distance, I could see Brandon leaning in close to that girl—Jess, the one who always wore skirts that were just short enough to skirt the dress code. His hands lingered on her thigh, his fingers inching higher, daring her to react. She didn't, of course. She giggled like it was the funniest thing in the world, leaning into his touch as if it validated her existence.

For a fleeting moment, Brandon's eyes met mine. His smirk deepened, and he winked in that smug, infuriating way of his. It wasn't flirtatious—not really. It was a performance. A declaration. *This is what real boys do.* His hand crept higher, and my stomach churned. I looked away, my hands curling into fists at my sides. The sting of his laughter from that bathroom replayed in my mind, echoing over and over again. I hated him. And yet, some twisted part of me still wanted his approval, still wished he'd come over and apologize, still craved that connection we used to have.

The final bell rang, and we shuffled into social studies with Mr. Donaldson. If there was ever a person I'd describe as a caricature of himself, it would be him. Scruffy hair, coffee-stained tie, and an air of superiority that was entirely unwarranted. He was less of a teacher and more of a gossip with a podium.

"Alright, let's settle down," he drawled, slapping a ruler against his desk for emphasis. "We've got an exciting topic today. *Human relationships.*" The class erupted into a mix of groans and stifled laughter. I braced myself, already dreading what was coming.

He paced the front of the room, hands clasped behind his back like he was delivering a sermon. "Now, there's been a lot of talk about relationships lately. Boys, girls... other arrangements." His eyes landed on me, a sly grin tugging at the corners of his mouth. "And I hear some of you have very... unique perspectives on the matter."

The room went silent. My classmates' heads turned in unison, their eyes boring into me like I was some exotic specimen under a microscope. My throat tightened, my hands gripping the edges of my desk so hard my knuckles turned white. I didn't say a word. I wouldn't give him the satisfaction.

"What's the matter?" he prodded. "Cat got your tongue?"

I stared back at him, unblinking, until the smugness on his face faltered. "That's enough, sir," I said quietly, but firmly. My voice didn't waver, and for once, I was grateful.

The tension in the room broke as quickly as it had formed. Marcus, the class clown, piped up with a laugh. "Buzzkill," he muttered under his breath, earning a ripple of laughter from the others. Was I supposed to allow myself to be taunted and crucified for their entertainment?— these kids are sick.

But I didn't care. I was already mentally checked out, counting down the minutes until I could escape this hellhole.

When the final bell rang, I bolted. My feet carried me out of the building and down the street, the autumn air biting at my cheeks. I didn't stop until I reached the park near my house, collapsing onto an empty bench. The weight of the day pressed down on me, suffocating and relentless.

I hated them. All of them. My classmates, my teachers, the entire godforsaken school. But most of all, I hated Brandon. I hated the way he made me feel—weak, humiliated, powerless. And yet, buried beneath all that anger was something far more unsettling. A flicker of something I didn't want to name. Something that scared me.

I pulled my knees to my chest, staring at the cracked pavement beneath my feet. I didn't know what to do, how to make it stop. The rumors, the teasing, the whispers—it was all too much. For the first time in my life, I felt completely and utterly alone.

But then, a thought crept into my mind, unbidden and unwelcome. *Revenge.*

It wasn't a plan, not yet. Just a seed, planted deep in the recesses of my mind. But as I sat there, staring into the fading light of the evening, that seed began to take root. Brandon had taken so much from me—my dignity, my peace of mind, my sense of safety. Maybe it was time I took something back.

ENTRY #13
6 October 2010

We got a new technology teacher, Ms. Sawyer. I was relatively excited, because our previous male teacher, Mr. Leurch, was not very audible and had a hard time conveying the lesson plans. He was a nice guy, but technology was my least favorite subject and my most challenging subject. I am more gifted in literature and the arts anyway.

Ms. Sawyer is a thirty-something beautiful redhead with piercing green eyes, and an enviable body— one that most of my male peers couldn't help but to fawn over— a disgusting bunch. I liked her from the onset, up until she rearranged our seats and wanted to sit us all with a partner.

Todd and Brandon were the first to volunteer to sit together at the far back— to no one's surprise. Sawyer immediately declined and established that she'd be the one to assign seats. As if my troubles couldn't intensify more— I was assigned a seat next to Brandon at the back. Todd was matched with the class goody-goody, Victoria.— a girl who seemingly can't do anything wrong.

I was uncomfortable, and a brief silence added to the awkwardness. We both looked in opposite directions. With Brandon making gag faces at Todd, seemingly implying how gross it is to sit next to me.

After the seat arrangements had concluded, Sawyer essentially made us cringily greet our deskmates as if we'd just met each other. I defiantly remained quiet— Brandon, on the other hand, let out a snark, "Let's try to get along, man-woman," before laughing at his own insult.

"Fuck you," I whispered to him angrily.

"Ew, you want to fuck me?" he responded condescendingly. "I always knew you were eyeing my ass, but you can forget about it, I'm a real man," he said.

I kept quiet.

I could feel the anger building inside me, but I forced it down, not wanting to give him the satisfaction of seeing me upset. The truth was, though, it was getting harder to ignore. The space next to him was now like an active battlefield—one that I'd have to navigate every day for the next two months. Two months. That's all I had to get through.

I tried focusing on the lesson, but I could feel Brandon's presence next to me. His scent—this mix of sweat, soap, and something distinctly him—kept distracting me. The absurdity of it all—he was the last person I wanted to be around, yet there I was, stuck next to him in silence for long stretches of time. At times, I could almost feel his gaze on me, just lingering in the periphery. I didn't dare to look at him, even when I felt his eyes trace the outline of my arm or fall on my hand.

There were moments where I caught myself sitting too still, almost holding my breath, as though every movement was under his scrutiny. Every breath he took seemed to feel like a weight on my chest. And when the lesson was over, he would turn his attention to Todd, sharing whispered jokes, and I would be forgotten again. That was fine by me. I didn't want his attention, especially not in the way he gave it.

But sometimes it wasn't that simple. He would brush against me when we were moving around the classroom, and I would feel it like a jolt of electricity. I would stiffen instinctively, but he seemed to enjoy that. I tried to pretend it didn't bother me, but the truth was, it unsettled me deeply. Maybe it was the way he acted as though he had power over me—his playful insults, his proximity.

It was strange, being in this liminal space with him. It wasn't hatred, not anymore. Maybe it had never been. It was something else, something harder to define—resentment mixed with a twisted sense of need, like I couldn't stop thinking about him even though I knew I should. I despised him, and yet, I found myself fixating on the way his muscles rippled under his shirt when he leaned over the desk. The subtle curve of his lips when he smiled at Todd. The laughter that seemed to make everyone else so eager to join in.

But I wasn't like them. I wasn't like Brandon, or Todd, or any of the others. I didn't need to belong. That was the lie I told myself every day.

I tried to keep my focus on the lessons, my mind drifting back to the things I actually enjoyed—books, art, writing—but I couldn't escape the constant pull of Brandon's presence. And that day, for the first time in a long time, I had a thought I couldn't push away: I hated him. I hated him more than anything.

ENTRY #14
20 December 2010

The holiday season was supposed to be my reprieve—a much-needed escape from the daily torment of school and those savage classmates. I'd started to regain some sense of calm, filling my days with reading, helping Gran around the house, and savoring the quiet. But, of course, life had other plans.

Coming back from a grocery run, arms weighed down with bags of essentials, I spotted them: Brandon and his father. They were moving into the decrepit block of flats just three houses down from ours. Even from the distance, it was impossible not to notice Brandon's body language—his shoulders slumped, his gaze fixed on the ground, like a dog beaten into submission. His father, towering and menacing, barked orders at him while lugging a battered suitcase from their rusted truck. For a fleeting second, I almost felt a pang of sympathy for Brandon, but the memory of his relentless bullying at school quickly snuffed it out.

A dark thought crossed my mind, unbidden but satisfying: *I hope his dad beats the life out of him.*

Gran, ever the community observer, filled me in on the backstory I hadn't asked for. Apparently, Brandon's father had been in prison for most of my elementary and middle school years—something about a violent assault on a woman. I wasn't surprised. One look at the man and you could tell he was dangerous. The kind of predator you'd instinctively cross the street to avoid. Gran warned me to steer clear of him, her tone unusually sharp. The entire neighborhood, it seemed, was terrified of this man, though they kept up a facade of forced politeness and hollow smiles whenever he was around.

"No one wants to be on his bad side," Gran muttered as she peeled potatoes for dinner. "But mark my words, child, there's evil in that family. You'd do well to keep your distance."

I didn't argue. It wasn't like I was planning to get chummy with Brandon or his twisted family. If anything, his father's arrival only deepened the mystery of why Brandon had turned out the way he did.

It wasn't just his father who raised eyebrows in the neighborhood. I'd recently learned, through the endless web of local gossip, that Brandon had an older sister. I'd never seen her before, but the whispers painted a sordid picture. She was said to be stunningly beautiful, but with a reputation as a prostitute. The rumors didn't stop there. The most horrifying claim, whispered in hushed tones and never openly acknowledged, was that her own father was one of her clients.

I wanted to believe it was nothing more than the twisted fabrications of bored neighbors, but something about it gnawed at me. The source of this particular revelation was one of the local police officers, a woman notorious for her loose lips and penchant for spreading every sordid detail she encountered on the job. Confidentiality was clearly not her strong suit, but no one in the community seemed to mind. If anything, they thrived on her stories, dissecting every word like vultures around a carcass.

The more I thought about it, the more it all made sense—or at least fit the narrative I'd constructed in my mind. Brandon wasn't just a bully; he was a product of something far darker. His cruelty at school, his fixation with degrading others—it all seemed like a desperate attempt to assert control in a life where he probably had none. But knowing that didn't soften my hatred for him. If anything, it made it worse. I didn't want to empathize with him or try to understand him. I wanted to see him suffer, the way he'd made me suffer.

That night, as I lay in bed, I couldn't stop replaying the scene from earlier in the day. Brandon's father barking at him, the way Brandon flinched at every word. It was strange seeing him like that, stripped of the bravado he wore like armor at school. For the first time, I saw a version of him that wasn't terrifying or hateful—just small and scared. It unsettled me more than I cared to admit.

But then I remembered the bathroom incident, the cruel laughter, the whispered taunts that had haunted me for weeks. I clenched my fists, feeling the familiar surge of anger rise in my chest. Brandon didn't deserve my sympathy. Not after what he'd done.

And yet, a part of me couldn't shake the feeling that there was more to him than I'd ever understand. A dark, tangled mess of secrets and pain that I wasn't sure I wanted to unravel.

ENTRY #15
26 JANUARY 2011

The beginning of a new school year always carries the same predictable undertones: the screeching of desk legs against tiled floors, the faint smell of disinfectant from freshly cleaned classrooms, and the teachers' voices layering threats about textbook acquisition deadlines. It's as if they get an annual script—filled with proclamations of how intolerant they are of nonsense, how we're "not babies anymore," and how this year will be the most difficult one yet. It's all a tedious ritual, but the monotony is oddly comforting, like the ticking of a reliable old clock.

Most of the same stuffy classmates from last year remain, as do the regular fixtures of my school-life misery: Todd and Brandon. They've only grown closer over the break, their "brotherhood" thicker than ever, and their synchronized torment sharper. It's like they'd spent the entire holiday practicing ways to be insufferable. I did my best to avoid them as the day dragged on, weaving through the hallways like prey avoiding a predator. But, as fate would have it, this year brought someone entirely new into the mix.

Her name was Pearl.

When she stepped into the classroom, all conversations ceased. Even Todd and Brandon, masters of disruption, seemed to falter in their usual barrage of crude jokes. Pearl wasn't just beautiful; she was *perfect*. Her skin was a warm tan, her features sharp and symmetrical as though they'd been sculpted by the gods themselves. Her hazel eyes carried a piercing intelligence, and her long, straight black hair fell in a cascade down her back, looking like it had never known a bad day. She was the epitome of every magazine cover cliché—but in the flesh.

Of course, my classmates' reactions were immediate and predictable. The boys were practically oozing testosterone, their hungry stares filling the air like smog. Some were already nudging each other and planning their strategies to flirt, while the girls exchanged glances filled with thinly veiled envy. I could feel the collective weight of the room's superficiality pressing down on me.

When Pearl was asked to choose a seat, she took her time scanning the classroom. My heart sank as I watched the boys puff out their chests and adjust their hair, each hoping to be her choice. And then, to my utter shock—and to everyone else's dismay—she chose the seat right next to me.

Me.

The class pariah.

The silence in the room turned deafening. Whispers started spreading, and I caught glimpses of disbelief on everyone's faces. The girls' envy shifted into something sharper, more pointed. The boys' confusion turned to irritation, as though my very presence beside her offended them.

But Pearl was unfazed by their reactions. She pulled out the chair beside me with a grace I could only envy, turned to me, and smiled.

"Hi, I'm Pearl. What's your name?" she asked warmly.

For a moment, I was too stunned to respond. Her voice was soft, inviting, entirely free of the condescension I'd grown used to.

"I... uh... hi! Nice to meetcha. I'm..." I stumbled over my words, my tongue tripping on itself before I finally managed to introduce myself.

Her smile widened. It wasn't the kind of smile people give when they're being polite. It was genuine, like she was actually happy to be sitting beside me.

As the day went on, I realized that Pearl wasn't just stunning; she was also grounded in a way most of my classmates weren't. While others in the room flaunted their personalities like costumes, Pearl seemed entirely comfortable in her own skin. She asked me about my interests, what books I liked, and whether I preferred drawing or writing. No one had ever shown that much interest in me before. It was... disarming.

At one point during the lesson, Brandon, seated a few rows behind us, leaned over to Todd and whispered something. They both laughed loudly, drawing attention to themselves as usual. Pearl turned briefly to look at them, her expression unreadable.

"They seem... lively," she remarked to me, her tone dripping with diplomacy.

"More like *annoying*," I muttered under my breath, though a small smile tugged at the corners of my lips.

Pearl chuckled softly. "Fair enough."

By the time the lunch bell rang, I was convinced that sitting next to Pearl might just make this year bearable.

The lunch break, however, was another story entirely.

I wasn't particularly social during lunch. My usual routine was to find a quiet corner of the yard, away from the chaos of the cliques and drama, and bury myself in a book. Today, however, Pearl sought me out before I could escape.

"Mind if I join you?" she asked, holding her tray.

"Uh... sure," I said, quickly scooting over to make space for her on the bench.

As we ate, we talked about everything and nothing. Pearl told me she'd moved here because her dad got a new job in town. She was nervous about starting at a new school but seemed to be handling it with remarkable grace. I found myself opening up to her about my love for art and my dreams of becoming an illustrator someday.

For the first time in what felt like forever, I wasn't on guard.

That changed when Brandon and Todd strolled by, their eyes immediately locking onto us.

"Well, well, well," Brandon drawled, his trademark smirk firmly in place. "If it isn't the odd couple."

Todd snickered, already anticipating whatever insult Brandon was about to lob.

"Guess we know why you didn't sit with any of the boys, Pearl," Brandon continued, his voice loud enough to draw attention from nearby tables. "Didn't want to hurt your little boyfriend's feelings, huh?"

I clenched my fists under the table, my appetite vanishing.

Pearl, however, didn't miss a beat.

"Better than sitting with someone who peaked in elementary school," she shot back, her tone sweet but her words razor-sharp.

The smirk dropped from Brandon's face, replaced by a brief flash of surprise before he recovered.

"Feisty," he said, but his voice lacked its usual confidence.

"Let's go," Todd muttered, tugging at Brandon's sleeve.

As they walked away, Pearl turned back to me, her expression calm.

"Sorry about that," she said.

I shook my head, still processing what had just happened. No one had ever stood up for me like that before.

ENTRY #16
8 February 2011

Over the next few weeks, Pearl and I became inseparable. She quickly earned a reputation as one of the smartest students in class, effortlessly outshining even the teacher's pets. Her presence seemed to shift the classroom dynamic, drawing attention away from the usual drama.

Brandon, however, didn't take kindly to being overshadowed.

During a group project in science class, he made it his mission to undermine Pearl at every turn. Whether it was making snide comments about her ideas or deliberately misinterpreting her instructions, he was relentless.

Pearl, to her credit, handled it with grace. She never rose to his bait, instead addressing his antics with a calm that only seemed to frustrate him further.

One afternoon, as we packed up our things after class, Brandon cornered us near the lockers.

"You think you're better than everyone, don't you?" he sneered at Pearl.

Pearl met his gaze evenly. "I don't think I'm better than everyone. Just you."

I barely had time to stifle my laughter before Brandon turned his glare on me.

"And you," he said, his voice low. "Don't think I've forgotten about you. You're still the same pathetic little nobody you've always been."

I didn't respond.

Pearl stepped between us. "Leave him alone, Brandon."

For a moment, I thought he was going to retaliate. His fists clenched at his sides, his face a mask of barely contained rage. But then Todd appeared, pulling him away with a muttered, "Not worth it, man."

As they disappeared down the hall, Pearl turned to me, her expression softening.

"You okay?" she asked.

"Yeah," I said, though my voice wavered slightly.

"You don't have to let him talk to you like that, you know," she said gently.

"I know," I replied.

But deep down, I wasn't so sure.

Pearl's presence in my life is a light I hadn't realized I needed. For the first time in years, I felt seen. She encouraged me to stand up for myself, to push back against the people who sought to tear me down.

And slowly, I began to believe her.

By the end of the school year, I'd found a strength I didn't know I had. Pearl and I weren't just friends; we were allies in a war against the cruelty of adolescence.

And for the first time, I felt like I might actually survive it.

ENTRY #17
1 April 2011

Today was a day unlike any other. For weeks, I've been reflecting on the identity others have forced upon me—the teasing, the rumors, the endless assumptions. It got me thinking: maybe, just maybe, it's time I take control of the narrative.

I woke up early, my heart pounding with the weight of the decision. I rummaged through my grandmother's old trunk, where she kept some of her 1970s vintage clothing. There it was: a floral-print maxi dress that still smelled faintly of lavender. I slipped it on, fumbling with the zipper, the fabric hugging me awkwardly in all the wrong places. A quick rummage through her makeup drawer left me armed with a tube of clumpy mascara and the brightest red lipstick I'd ever seen.

Staring at my reflection in the mirror, I felt a surge of courage. "This is me," I thought, standing tall, clutching a small faux-leather purse.

I strutted out the door, avoiding my grandmother's curious eyes. "You'll catch a cold in that," she said, mistaking my ensemble for a poor attempt at fashion rather than a bold statement.

The walk to school was nerve-wracking. Every car that passed felt like it slowed just a fraction too long. The whispers started the moment I entered the schoolyard. Gasps, snickers, and wide-eyed stares.

I ignored them. Today was my day.

The first bell rang, and I made a beeline for the girl's bathroom. The shocked squeals and the chorus of "What the heck?!" from inside only confirmed I'd made an impression.

Just kidding.

It's April Fools' Day. Of course, I didn't dress up like a woman or sashay my way into the girls' restroom!

Instead, I sat in the back of class, as usual, quietly plotting ways to survive another week of middle school drama. But hey, at least I got you for a second, didn't I? Maybe there's a lesson in this: don't believe everything you read—or hear—on a day dedicated to fooling people.

For now, I'll stick to dressing how I normally do, letting my eccentricities shine in subtler, less lipstick-heavy ways. But it's fun to imagine the chaos that kind of prank could cause. Maybe next year.

Until then, I'll settle for planting a stink bomb in Brandon and Todd's lockers. Now that's a prank worth executing.

ENTRY #18
2 May 2011

After a careless remark about Todd and Brandon's unsettlingly close friendship, I've unexpectedly found myself growing incredibly close to Pearl. It's a friendship that feels both refreshing and revolutionary, a bond strong enough to rattle the sneers and gossip of my classmates. Together, we've become almost inseparable, much to the dismay of those who hoped she'd fall victim to their whispered warnings about my so-called "homosexual tendencies."

The boys have tried—repeatedly and shamelessly—to dissuade Pearl from associating with me. They've fed her stories, exaggerated my supposed "otherness," and issued vague, unsolicited "warnings" about my character. But she hasn't wavered. Instead, Pearl stands by me with a loyalty I hadn't experienced since Suzy in elementary school. Her unwavering support feels like armor, shielding me from the ridicule that used to sting so sharply.

Beyond friendship, her presence has catalyzed changes I didn't think were possible.

For starters, my grades have improved significantly. Pearl's discipline and meticulousness have rubbed off on me. She doesn't just study—she *masters* the material, and she's encouraged me to do the same. What once seemed like insurmountable obstacles in subjects like mathematics and science have now become manageable, even enjoyable at times. I've started to take pride in my work, something I hadn't done in years. Last week, for the first time ever, I scored the highest in class on a social studies test—a subject dominated by those I'd rather not name. The look on Todd's face when the teacher announced my name was priceless.

With Pearl's influence, I've also grown braver in facing the insults hurled by my classmates. It's not that the taunts have disappeared—far from it—but they've lost their power. When someone calls me a name or snickers behind my back, I've begun responding with wit, sarcasm, or sometimes a cold, disinterested stare. It's a game to them, and nothing deflates a bully's ego faster than realizing they're not getting the reaction they crave. Pearl often laughs at my comebacks, her approval bolstering my confidence.

Brandon, however, seems to have noticed the shift in my demeanor—and in my friendship with Pearl.

He's been attempting, albeit shallowly, to worm his way into my good graces. On more than one occasion, he's approached me with forced smiles and transparently insincere small talk. "Hey, man, how's it going?" he'll ask, as though our history of animosity never existed. I'm not stupid. It's painfully obvious what he's after.

Pearl.

He doesn't even try to hide his fascination with her. During class, his eyes frequently drift in her direction, his smirk betraying whatever calculated thoughts are running through his head. And when he isn't ogling her, he's attempting to bait me into conversation—desperate to extract whatever information he can.

"Hey, so, Pearl's really cool, huh?" he said just the other day, leaning casually against my desk like we were old pals.

"Cooler than you'll ever be," I retorted, not even looking up from my notebook.

His smug expression faltered for a moment before he regained his composure. "Relax, man. I'm just saying, she seems chill. You're lucky to have her as a friend."

The way he emphasized the word "friend" made my skin crawl. He wasn't just trying to infiltrate—he was attempting to demean what Pearl and I had, reducing it to something shallow and trivial. But his attempts only served to deepen my resolve.

Pearl, for her part, seems oblivious to Brandon's schemes, or perhaps she simply doesn't care. She's far too intelligent to fall for his charm, even if he did manage to worm his way closer. Still, I can't help but feel a sense of protectiveness over her. She's the first true friend I've had in years, and I'll be damned if I let Brandon or anyone else tarnish that.

This friendship—unexpected, unwavering, and fiercely loyal—has given me something I haven't felt in a long time: hope. Hope that I'm more than the labels they try to pin on me. Hope that the world isn't entirely full of people like Brandon and Todd.

And, for the first time in what feels like forever, I believe I can stand my ground.

ENTRY #19

11 July 2011

Today was a particularly disgusting day. We had an assignment due—build a house out of recyclable materials. Everyone was scurrying around with their projects, filling the technology class with their creations to be graded. I made a simple townhouse out of tin foil and recycled fiberglass.

B randon and Todd, to no one's surprise, didn't submit theirs because they 'forgot.' I paid them no mind. Today, Pearl had called in sick and asked me to submit a sick note on her behalf with a promise to submit the project ASAP. I offered to submit it for her, but being the perfectionist she is, she insisted on submitting it herself. Nothing was going to change my mind.

I never thought this seemingly exciting day would end so disastrously. Brandon had devised a petty and repulsive plan to ruin it for me.

Aside from the building I created, I had also made novelty trees outside for decoration. I dropped off my project at the technology class, alongside the others, and went about my day. From a distance, I could see Brandon being scolded after attempting to make another excuse for not submitting his project on time. He then turned his gaze toward me, with intent.

A random girl from another class who had submitted her project around the same time I did came to notify me that she noticed some of my novelty assets were missing before my project was graded. I immediately suspected and confronted Brandon. The intentional glare he gave me was unsettling, as if he was expecting me. He softly told me to follow him to the bathroom.

After much resistance, he finally convinced me to follow him there, where I immediately demanded my assets back. What happened next was beyond my worst expectations. After a brief tussle, I tried searching his pockets for my missing assets but had no success. Brandon smugly told me the assets were "inside him," which took me a while to understand. Yes, that's right—he had stuffed my novelty assets inside his anus and was now more than willing to hand them over to me.

Throwing subtle jabs after my visceral reaction and rejection of them, he said, "Don't you want them anymore? I thought you wanted to take them back." He then added, "Don't worry, I know you always wanted to dig into my butt."

It was another attempt at baiting and degrading me. Thankfully, Todd wasn't there, so I could freely confront Brandon about his sickening actions.

"Why are you doing this?" I asked. "Why do you hate me like this?"

This prompted Brandon to casually reply, "Because your kind is not welcome here."

That was a lie. His hatred for me ran far deeper than he was letting on.

I had never been so enraged. I got physical with him, something I had never done before. In a fit of rage, I tugged on his shirt, creasing it.

"Look at the lady fighting back," he said coldly. "Let go, gay-boy."

Naturally, I asked what his problem with me was.

After what felt like forever, he responded with a silent, "You abandoned me and threw me to the wolves." He then added, "Now I can't be held responsible for my future actions."

Those words were frightening and foreboding. I had no idea what he meant by that.

After Brandon's cryptic words, I was left standing in that bathroom, still seething but confused. What had he meant by that? What did he think I'd abandoned him for? As much as I wanted to press him further, my instincts told me to walk away. I was more shaken than I wanted to admit.

I left the bathroom, trying to collect myself, but it was no use. My mind was spinning. Brandon's actions were vile, but what he'd said—those last words—lingered in my head. "I can't be held responsible for my future actions." It felt like a threat, but I couldn't figure out what he meant by it. Was it a warning, or was he just trying to mess with me, like he always did?

The rest of the day passed in a blur. I barely heard anything in class, distracted by the image of Brandon's smirk and the coldness in his eyes. It was as if, for a moment, I had seen something deeper in him—something that wasn't just cruelty, but a twisted kind of bitterness, a bitterness that had festered for years.

When I got home, I tried to shake it off, but every time I closed my eyes, I saw Brandon's face, his smug expression. I kept wondering if he was playing some sick game with me, or if there was some deeper, darker meaning behind his words. I tried to talk to Pearl about it, but she was busy with her own things, and I didn't want to burden her with yet another problem. So, I kept it to myself, a growing knot of unease in my stomach.

Days passed, and I kept thinking about Brandon. I couldn't figure him out. One moment, he was tormenting me, and the next, it was like he was trying to make some sort of connection. What was his deal? Was he playing a game, trying to manipulate me? Or was he genuinely that messed up? Either way, I couldn't let him control me. I'd been through too much already to let him pull me back into his web of nonsense.

But the more I thought about it, the more I realized something. There was no way I could just forget about what had happened. The things Brandon had said—those words were too significant, too strange, to ignore.

Maybe it was time to confront him again. Maybe it was time to get some answers. I didn't know what I was going to say, but I couldn't leave things like this. I had to find out what Brandon really meant, and why he had made my life so miserable for so long.

But would he even tell me the truth?

Interlude: The Conversation with Brandon

The room was quiet now, save for the rhythmic hum of the fluorescent lights above. The sterile scent of old textbooks and cleaning supplies lingered in the air, a smell I would later associate with this place, with this moment. I stared at the faded calendar on the wall, my fingers curling around the edge of my coffee cup as I waited for Brandon. The conversation we were about to have was long overdue, though neither of us would admit that aloud.

He entered the room with his usual swagger, shoulders broad and confident, his expression unreadable. As he made his way across the floor, the room seemed to shrink. The air grew thick with the weight of what was unsaid between us, the history we had shared, the petty, juvenile games we had played, and the betrayal that had cut deeper than I would ever let on.

"Nice place," Brandon remarked as he lowered himself into the chair opposite me. He sat with his legs spread wide, like he owned the space, like he owned everything around him. He was still the same Brandon, the same arrogant, untouchable force he'd always been. His eyes flickered to me briefly before returning to the room around him, as though unsure of how to navigate this new version of me—this me that wasn't the same kid he'd tormented years ago.

I didn't reply immediately. Instead, I studied him. His clothes were more expensive now, more fitted, more refined. He was taller, broader, his jawline sharper—he looked almost too polished for the guy I used to know. But beneath all the changes, there was still that undeniable edge. That hunger. And, perhaps, a touch of vulnerability that I wasn't sure was intentional or just a side effect of growing up.

"I see you're still with Todd," I finally said, my tone casual but edged with the slightest hint of something darker.

Brandon's lips quirked upward, his eyes flicking toward mine. "What's that supposed to mean?" he asked, his voice light but with an undercurrent I recognized too well. It was the same defensiveness he'd always had, a shield against anything that threatened his carefully curated persona.

"Nothing," I said, leaning back in my chair. "Just that you two are still... inseparable." The words were dipped in sarcasm, but I masked them with a smile I knew he would misread.

He laughed, the sound shallow and too practiced. "You're still hung up on that, huh? Thought you'd grown out of it by now."

I wasn't sure if he was referring to the past or to the fact that I was sitting here with him in the first place. Either way, the jab didn't sting as much as it used to. Maybe that's what bothered me.

"I don't think I ever really grew out of anything," I replied, voice steady, though the implication hung between us like a broken thread. "Just adapted. We all have to."

Brandon shifted in his seat, his eyes narrowing as he processed the meaning behind my words. He wasn't an idiot, despite the impression he liked to give. He leaned forward, elbows on his knees, hands clasped together like he was trying to negotiate a deal. "You sound like one of those self-help books or some shit," he said, his lips pulling into a grin that didn't reach his eyes.

I didn't smile back. I knew better than to offer him that satisfaction. "You're the one who came here for advice, Brandon," I said quietly, my gaze never leaving his.

There it was. A shift. For the first time in years, I saw something like uncertainty flicker in his eyes. It lasted only a moment, but it was enough for me to know that, whatever game he was playing, it was beginning to unravel.

"Yeah, well," he muttered, leaning back in his chair again, trying to reclaim some of his bravado, "I just wanted to see how you're doing. Haven't seen you around much."

It was almost laughable how fake his concern sounded. He wasn't really interested in my well-being. He was more interested in putting himself back in the driver's seat. The old Brandon had always been about control, about pulling the strings behind the scenes, and I knew that if he thought he could worm his way back into my life, he would.

"Everything's fine," I said, cutting through the tension. "Life's good. I don't need anything from you."

Brandon's eyes flickered briefly to the floor before coming back to meet mine. His voice dropped, taking on a more serious tone, though the deflection was still there. "You know, I heard about some of the stuff you've been doing. You're not exactly... invisible."

I raised an eyebrow, curious despite myself. "What are you talking about?"

"Just," he paused, glancing away as though measuring his words, "you're kind of a legend now. People talk." He let the words hang in the air, like they were meant to mean something more than they did. But I wasn't biting.

"So what?" I said, pushing the edge of my coffee cup back and forth across the desk. "People talk about a lot of things. But I don't need to hear it from you."

Brandon snorted, clearly irritated by my dismissal. "You know, you've got a funny way of acting like you're too good for all this." His eyes flickered with something that was almost resentment, though it quickly turned back into a forced smirk. "I get it. You think you're better than me now. Or maybe you're just scared of me. Is that it?"

It was like a flicker of something—a challenge, a dare. And for the first time in a long time, I was ready to meet it head-on. "I'm not scared of you, Brandon. I'm just bored of you."

That got a reaction. His lips pressed together, and for a moment, he looked like he might snap. But he didn't. He couldn't. Because beneath all that bravado, beneath all the layers of arrogance and deflection, he knew the truth. And that truth was that we were no longer the same.

"Fine," he said after a pause, his voice a little lower now. "I didn't come here for a fight."

"Then what did you come here for?" I asked, genuinely curious now, my arms crossed.

Brandon hesitated, the mask slipping for just a fraction of a second. "I don't know," he admitted, the vulnerability in his voice almost imperceptible. "Maybe I just wanted to... make things right. Or at least... make it better between us."

I didn't respond right away. Instead, I studied him—really looked at him. The old Brandon, the one I had known so well, was gone. Or at least, it was fading. I wasn't sure what was replacing him, but whatever it was, it wasn't someone I wanted to be around.

"You can't just undo the past," I said, my voice cold. "You can't just walk back in here like nothing happened."

Brandon didn't argue. Instead, he let out a frustrated breath and rubbed his face. "I know," he muttered, "but I had to try."

I stood up then, the conversation over in my mind. There was nothing left to say, nothing more to salvage. "You tried," I said, offering him a brief glance as I gathered my things. "But I'm not your redemption project, Brandon."

He didn't stop me as I walked toward the door, but his voice trailed after me, soft and uncharacteristically earnest. "I didn't want to be."

I paused at the door, looking back at him one last time. "Then don't," I said. "Just leave me out of it."

With that, I stepped out of the room, the door clicking softly behind me, and I left Brandon to ponder whatever it was he had hoped to find in this moment. The truth was, he'd already lost me. And no amount of words—no matter how many times he tried to weave them into something meaningful—could ever change that.

ENTRY #20
15 July 2011

Today marked one of the most exhausting and yet satisfying days of my school life. I couldn't keep what Brandon had done to me bottled up any longer. The memory of his smug, condescending remarks and his grotesque actions wouldn't stop replaying in my mind. It was as if his voice was taunting me, daring me to stay silent. But Gran's stern and unwavering belief in justice pushed me forward.

I sat across from her at the kitchen table last night, nervously recounting every vile detail of Brandon's behavior: the stolen project pieces, the degrading encounter in the bathroom, and his sinister words about my "kind" not being welcome. Her face betrayed a mixture of horror and fury, and she didn't hesitate to say what I already knew deep down.

"This has gone on long enough," she said, her tone firm but comforting. "You have to tell someone, and not just for yourself. Who knows what else that boy's been doing to others?"

The thought hadn't occurred to me before. Could Brandon have been tormenting others too? And if so, how many people had stayed silent, just as I had?

The next morning, I went straight to Ms. Sawyer, my technology teacher, before class began. It wasn't easy to recount everything, especially the humiliating parts, but her concern was genuine. She listened intently, her expression shifting from shock to disgust. By the time I finished, she assured me she would escalate the matter to the principal.

Little did I know, my complaint would open the floodgates.

The principal's office was packed. Brandon sat in the center of the room, his usual arrogance replaced with a thinly veiled unease. His eyes darted around, probably sizing up everyone present to see who might turn against him. Todd sat beside him, looking uncharacteristically tense. The room buzzed with whispers until the principal called for silence.

"Today, we are addressing a very serious matter," he began, his voice stern. "This school has a zero-tolerance policy for bullying, harassment, or inappropriate behavior of any kind. I expect complete honesty from everyone involved."

What started as an inquiry into my accusations quickly snowballed into a full-blown investigation.

The first bombshell came from one of the quieter girls in our class, a timid student named Emily. She stood up hesitantly, her voice trembling as she recounted how Brandon had cornered her during a school trip, making inappropriate comments and touching her without consent. The room fell silent, the weight of her words hanging in the air.

Then another girl, Sarah, spoke up, followed by two more. Each story added to the growing list of grievances against Brandon. A few boys even chimed in, detailing incidents where Brandon had slapped them on the back of the head or made crude jokes about their bodies during gym class.

For the first time, Brandon's confidence seemed to waver. He leaned back in his chair, crossing his arms defensively, his smirk faltering. But when he finally spoke, his response was as vile as ever.

"They're lying," he said, his voice dripping with disdain. "They just hate me because I'm popular and they're not."

The principal raised an eyebrow, clearly unimpressed. "This is not a popularity contest, Brandon. These are serious allegations, and dismissing them won't make them go away."

Realizing that his usual bravado wasn't going to work, Brandon tried a different tactic: deflection.

"Well, Todd was there for most of it," he said, pointing to his so-called best friend. "If I'm guilty, then so is he."

Todd's reaction was immediate. His face turned bright red, and he jumped to his feet, glaring at Brandon with a mix of anger and disbelief.

"Are you kidding me?" Todd shouted, his voice cracking. "I wasn't even there for half the stuff they're talking about! You're just trying to drag me down with you because you're too much of a coward to take responsibility for your actions!"

The tension between them was palpable, and for a moment, it seemed like they might come to blows right there in the principal's office. The principal quickly intervened, ordering them both to sit down.

Watching their friendship unravel was oddly satisfying. For years, they'd been inseparable, tormenting anyone who crossed their path. Seeing Todd finally stand up to Brandon felt like justice in its own way.

Pearl, who had been sitting quietly for most of the meeting, finally spoke up.

"I think it's clear who's responsible here," she said, her voice steady and unwavering. "Brandon's been bullying people for years, and he's gotten away with it because everyone's been too scared to stand up to him. But that ends today."

Her words seemed to ignite a spark in the room. One by one, more students came forward, sharing their own experiences. Even those who had been silent up until now found the courage to speak out.

But Brandon wasn't going down without a fight.

"You're all pathetic," he sneered, glaring at his classmates. "Do you think this is going to change anything? You're just jealous because you'll never be as good as me."

His attempts to intimidate us were laughable. The tide had turned, and no one was buying into his facade anymore.

When it was finally my turn to speak, I looked Brandon straight in the eye.

"You can try to intimidate us all you want, but it's not going to work," I said, my voice surprisingly steady. "This is the end of the line for you, Brandon. You've hurt too many people for too long, and we're not going to let you get away with it anymore."

The room fell silent. For the first time, Brandon had nothing to say.

After the meeting, as I walked out of the principal's office with Pearl by my side, I felt a sense of relief wash over me. For the first time, it felt like Brandon's reign of terror was truly over.

"You did good in there," Pearl said, giving me a reassuring smile.

"So did you," I replied.

As we walked down the hall, I couldn't help but think about how far I'd come. A few months ago, I never would have had the courage to stand up to someone like Brandon. But now, with the support of my friends and classmates, I finally felt like I could face anything.

And as for Brandon? Well, his downfall is only just beginning, and this time I will show him no mercy!

ENTRY #21
4 August 2011

Brandon returned today after his suspension, and the school felt like it was holding its collective breath. Whispers about his absence had swirled for weeks, ranging from speculation about reform school to rumors of brutal punishments at home. Whatever the truth was, it had clearly left its mark on him.

When he arrived at school, his usual scruffy appearance had somehow taken a turn for the worse. His uniform was wrinkled and poorly buttoned, and faint bruises were still visible on his face. He looked more disheveled and withdrawn than ever before.

Before coming to class, he reported to the principal's office as required. Those of us waiting in the hallway exchanged curious glances, straining to catch even a word of the conversation behind the closed door. But when Brandon finally emerged, he didn't acknowledge anyone. His face was blank, his posture rigid, and his pace steady as he made his way to our Bible study class.

The moment he entered, the atmosphere in the room shifted. The usual buzz of conversation and laughter died instantly, replaced by a heavy, unnerving silence. Brandon didn't meet anyone's gaze as he made his way to the back of the room and took a seat.

Our teacher, Mrs. Renshaw, paused mid-sentence, her eyes narrowing slightly as she took in his presence. "Welcome back, Brandon," she said carefully. "Please take out your materials and join us."

Without a word, he pulled out his worn Bible and placed it on the desk. His movements were methodical, almost robotic, and his face betrayed no emotion. For the rest of the lesson, he sat motionless, his eyes fixed on the pages in front of him.

At one point, Mrs. Renshaw called on him to read a passage aloud. The entire class stiffened, waiting to see how he would respond. Slowly, Brandon stood, opened his Bible, and began to read. His voice was steady, almost monotone, but there was something unsettling about it—an edge that sent a chill down my spine. It was as if he were reciting the words out of obligation, devoid of faith or understanding.

When he finished, Mrs. Renshaw nodded curtly and moved on without comment. Brandon sat down, folding his hands on his desk and staring ahead as though nothing had happened.

The eerie silence lingered even after class ended. Brandon was the first to leave, slipping out the door without waiting for Todd or any of his usual hangers-on. He didn't look at anyone, and no one dared to speak to him.

As Pearl and I gathered our things, she leaned in close. "Something's different about him," she whispered. "He's not the same."

I nodded, unable to disagree. Brandon's absence hadn't softened him; if anything, it had hardened him into something colder, more dangerous.

The rumors about his suspension continued to circulate. Some claimed he'd been sent to a correctional facility, where he'd been forced to fight for survival. Others speculated that his father had punished him brutally, taking out his frustration in violent ways. A few even suggested that Brandon had been involved in something truly dark and unspeakable during his time away.

Whatever had happened, it had left its mark. Brandon's silence was more unnerving than any of his past antics. It wasn't the silence of someone who had learned their lesson; it was the silence of someone biding their time, waiting for the right moment to strike.

"Mark my words," Pearl said as we walked to our next class. "This isn't over. He's planning something. You can see it in his eyes."

I didn't want to believe her, but...

INTERLUDE

The room feels unnervingly quiet, save for the soft buzz of the recorder. I lean forward slightly, locking eyes with Brandon, who sits across the table. His demeanor is casual, almost bored, but his gaze sharpens the moment I speak.

"So," I start, careful to keep my tone neutral, "what really happened during your suspension?"

Brandon shifts in his chair, a smirk tugging at the corner of his mouth. "Finally asking, huh? Guess you couldn't resist."

"I noticed the change when you came back," I reply evenly. "It wasn't like you to go so quiet."

He snorts softly, shaking his head. "Quiet? That's what you noticed? You've always been good at missing the point."

"Then enlighten me," I say, folding my hands on the table.

Brandon leans back, tilting his head as though considering how much to say. "You think suspension was a break? A time-out where I sat around playing video games and sulking? Nah. It was survival."

His words hang in the air, heavy with implication. I don't flinch, but my silence encourages him to continue.

"My old man wasn't thrilled about the school calling him up," Brandon says, his voice dipping into something darker. "Let's just say he didn't appreciate the 'embarrassment.' So when I walked through that door, he made damn sure I wouldn't forget who was boss."

"He hurt you," I say quietly, not posing it as a question.

Brandon laughs—a dry, humorless sound. "Hurt? Sure. Let's go with that. He got creative this time. Said I needed to learn a real lesson." He pauses, his eyes narrowing as if daring me to ask for details.

"And did you?" I ask, holding his gaze.

He doesn't answer right away. Instead, he leans forward, resting his elbows on the table. "I learned that no one's coming to save you. Not the school, not your friends, and sure as hell not your family. You deal with it, or you don't."

"That's why you came back... colder," I say, piecing the puzzle together.

Brandon shrugs, his smirk returning. "Colder, smarter, meaner—take your pick. It doesn't matter."

"What about Todd?" I press. "You didn't reconnect with him after that."

Brandon's smirk fades. His jaw tightens for just a moment before he answers. "Todd made his choice when he didn't stand by me. He was out. Simple as that."

"And the others? The people you... hurt?"

He meets my eyes, his expression unreadable. "Collateral. If you think I cared about their feelings back then, you've got the wrong guy."

There's no remorse in his tone, no trace of regret. But beneath the bravado, I catch a flicker of something—maybe anger, maybe shame, maybe both.

"What about now?" I ask softly. "Do you still see it that way?"

Brandon doesn't answer immediately. His fingers drum against the table, his gaze shifting as though he's weighing his next words. "Now?" he repeats. "Now, I see that it didn't matter. Not to them, not to you, not to anyone. What's done is done."

The weight of his words presses down on the room, and for a moment, neither of us speaks. Finally, I lean back, exhaling slowly.

"Thanks for answering," I say, my voice steady.

Brandon chuckles, shaking his head. "Yeah, sure. Let's call it a favor. But don't think you're getting anything more."

He leans back in his chair, his smirk returning, but it feels hollow now. Whatever walls he's built, they're thicker than I realized, and I'm not sure if I'll ever get through.

ENTRY #22
14 February 2012

Valentine's Day was always a strange ritual in middle school—a blend of forced sentimentality and awkward, half-hearted gestures. This year wasn't much different. The halls were an explosion of red and pink, the usual chaos of crumpled notes and overstuffed gift bags shoved into lockers. Every so often, a giggling group of girls would flit by, squealing about some grand confession or chocolate-filled bouquet. It wasn't my scene, but I couldn't help watching from the sidelines, as if I were waiting for some absurd plot twist to unfold.

Pearl, though, managed to make the day feel less suffocating. In the morning, she slipped me a single, heart-shaped chocolate. "Happy Valentine's Day," she said casually, as if it were no big deal. I could tell it was, though—she wasn't the type to waste gestures on people who didn't matter to her.

"Thanks," I muttered, feeling awkward but grateful. It wasn't a grand declaration, just a small act of kindness that cut through the noise of the day. That's who Pearl was, always finding ways to ground me when the world felt too chaotic.

The rest of the day, though, was anything but grounding. The air in the school was thick with tension, though I couldn't quite figure out why at first. It wasn't just the usual Valentine's

Day drama—though there was plenty of that. The whispers about Brandon had started up again, louder and more unsettling than before.

"I heard he's been sneaking around with Jenna," one girl said as I passed the lockers between classes.

Another voice chimed in, "She told Sarah he gave her something. You know, that new stuff going around."

I didn't need to ask what "that new stuff" was. *Euphoria.* The name had been splashed across the front pages of the local papers for weeks now, a party drug that was supposedly sweeping through the community. The articles were filled with vague warnings and stories of teens collapsing at house parties, their faces pale and unresponsive. It was the kind of thing that felt distant, like it belonged to some other town, some other group of kids.

Except now it didn't.

By lunchtime, the whispers had evolved into full-blown rumors. Brandon wasn't just sneaking around with Jenna, people said—he was dealing. I didn't know how much of it to believe, but the thought of him tied up in something like that didn't feel far-fetched.

He sat alone at lunch that day, his usual smirk absent. His posture was hunched, his head bent low over his tray like he was trying to make himself smaller. But even then, he managed to radiate that same unsettling energy, the kind that made it hard to look away.

I tried not to stare, but at one point, his gaze flicked up and caught mine. It was a split-second connection, but it was enough. His eyes were dark, almost hollow, but there was something else there too—something sharp and calculating.

I quickly turned back to my sandwich, pretending not to notice, but the moment lingered in my mind for the rest of the day.

By the time the final bell rang, the air felt heavier, as if the whole school was holding its breath. On the way out, I passed the newsstand on the corner and saw yet another headline about *Euphoria*. The picture beneath it showed a crumpled plastic baggie with a bright, glittering powder inside.

The walk home felt longer than usual. I couldn't shake the sense that something was shifting, that the fragile balance we'd all been clinging to in our final year of middle school was about to tip. Brandon's presence loomed over everything, even when he wasn't around.

When I got home, I pulled out the chocolate Pearl had given me. I stared at it for a long time before finally unwrapping it and popping it into my mouth. It was sweet, almost too sweet, but it brought a small smile to my face. For a moment, it reminded me that not everything in the world was dark or twisted.

But then I thought about Brandon again, and Jenna, and the whispers about *Euphoria*.

This was supposed to be our last year of middle school, a time to look forward to high school and new beginnings. Instead, it felt like we were all standing on the edge of something, staring into the unknown. And I can't help but wonder who among us was about to fall.

ENTRY #23
5 March 2012

Mondays were always sluggish, but today felt particularly heavy, as though the air itself was weighed down by something unseen. The lingering effects of Valentine's Day gossip and the unsettling rumors about *Euphoria* had not dissipated. If anything, they'd grown, mutating into something darker.

Pearl walked beside me as we made our way to first period. She was unusually quiet, her usual lighthearted banter replaced by a furrowed brow. "Did you hear?" she finally asked, her voice low, almost conspiratorial.

"Hear what?" I asked, bracing myself.

"Jenna. She didn't show up today. Apparently, she collapsed at a party over the weekend. They think it was... you know."

Euphoria. The word hung unspoken between us, heavy and accusing.

I felt a chill run down my spine. Jenna wasn't someone I'd ever been particularly close to, but the idea of her being caught up in something so dangerous—and so close to us—felt surreal. "Is she okay?" I asked, though I wasn't sure I wanted to know the answer.

"Hospitalized," Pearl said, shaking her head. "They're saying she's lucky to be alive."

The day passed in a strange haze, the usual monotony of classes overshadowed by whispers and half-truths. By lunch, the rumors had reached a fever pitch. People were pointing fingers, making accusations. Brandon's name came up more than once.

I spotted him across the cafeteria, sitting alone as he often did these days. He seemed unfazed by the attention—or maybe he just didn't care. His shoulders were hunched, his head low, but there was a tension in his posture, like a coiled spring ready to snap.

"Do you think it's true?" Pearl asked as we sat down with our trays.

"What?" I asked, though I knew exactly what she meant.

"That he's dealing. The stuff Jenna took."

I hesitated. "I don't know. It wouldn't surprise me, but... it feels too easy, you know? Like everyone just wants someone to blame."

Pearl nodded thoughtfully, but her eyes stayed fixed on Brandon. "Still, he's not exactly innocent."

The rest of the day dragged on, a strange mix of normalcy and unease. By the time the final bell rang, I felt drained, as though I'd been carrying a weight all day.

On the walk home, I couldn't stop thinking about Brandon. About the rumors. About Jenna. It was all connected somehow, but the pieces didn't quite fit.

Entry #24
10 March 2012

Athletics Day—just the thought of it sent a wave of dread coursing through me as soon as I woke up this morning. The very idea of spending an entire day outside, baking in the sun while pretending to care about running, jumping, or throwing things, was enough to make me wish I'd come down with a sudden case of the flu. But, of course, Gran was having none of it. "It's good for you to get out there," she said as she handed me my packed lunch. Good for who, though? Certainly not me.

The field was already teeming with students by the time I arrived. Brightly colored team shirts dotted the expanse of green like some misguided art project. Teachers barked instructions while groups of kids huddled together, laughing and cheering. I found myself hanging back, reluctant to dive into the chaos.

I've always hated sports days. It's not just the sweating and exertion—it's the exposure. The way everyone's watching, judging. You're either fast or slow, strong or weak, and there's no way to hide in the middle of a hundred-meter dash.

To make matters worse, Athletics Day has its own brand of awkward appeal. Some of the boys look like they've been carved out of marble, muscles flexing under the short sleeves of their jerseys, legs toned and tanned. I try not to stare, but it's impossible not to notice. It's mortifying, really, catching myself fawning over them like some lovesick fool. My eyes linger longer than they should, my mind wandering to places I'd rather not admit even to myself.

But I have my ways of escaping the day's worst tortures. I slip behind the bleachers, ducking out of sight when the teacher calls for volunteers for the hurdles. The air smells of grass and sweat, mingled with the faint chemical tang of the paint marking the lanes on the track. It's quieter here, away from the shouting and cheering.

Pearl eventually finds me, clutching a can of soda and looking just as disinterested in the whole affair as I feel. "Hiding, are we?" she asks, smirking as she plops down beside me.

"Obviously," I reply, rolling my eyes.

We spend the next hour people-watching, making snide comments about the overenthusiastic sprinters and the teachers who seem to think they're coaching the Olympics. It's the only part of Athletics Day I ever enjoy—being on the sidelines with Pearl, finding humor in the absurdity of it all.

As the afternoon wore on, I noticed Brandon lingering on the far side of the field, near the fence that separated the school grounds from the parking lot. He wasn't wearing his team shirt and seemed completely disinterested in the events, which wasn't unusual for him. What caught my attention, though, was the small group of girls gathered around him—none of them from our school.

They looked older, maybe high schoolers, with heavy makeup and short skirts that seemed wildly out of place at a school event. Brandon was leaning casually against the fence, talking to them in that low, almost lazy tone of his that always seemed to carry a hint of menace.

And then I saw it. A small pink pill in his hand, held out between two fingers like an offering. One of the girls took it, giggling nervously, while her friend hesitated before following suit.

My stomach churned. I couldn't look away as he leaned in closer to one of them, his hand brushing against her hip. She squirmed but didn't move away, and I felt a sickening mixture of anger and helplessness.

"What are you staring at?" Pearl's voice snapped me out of my trance.

"It's Brandon," I said, my voice low.

She followed my gaze and frowned. "What's he up to now?"

I didn't answer. I didn't need to. The scene unfolding in front of us was answer enough.

At one point, he reached out and grabbed one of the girls by the waist, pulling her closer. She laughed, but it sounded forced, her body stiff as his hand slid down her side.

I felt a surge of anger, my fists clenching at my sides. Pearl noticed and placed a hand on my arm. "Don't," she said quietly.

"What am I supposed to do?" I hissed. "Just stand here and watch?"

Pearl didn't reply, her eyes locked on the scene before us.

Eventually, the girls wandered off, giggling and glancing back at Brandon, who lit a cigarette and watched them go with a smirk.

Pearl and I exchanged a look.

"We can't keep ignoring this," I said finally, my voice trembling with a mix of fear and frustration.

"No, we can't," she agreed, her tone grim.

As much as I hated Athletics Day, it was nothing compared to the unease now settling in my chest. The rest of the afternoon passed in a blur, the cheers and laughter of my classmates fading into background noise. I couldn't shake the image of those girls, the pink pill, and Brandon's predatory smirk.

By the time the day ended, I felt drained, not from running or jumping or throwing things, but from the weight of what I'd seen—and the knowledge that it wouldn't be the last time.

By the late afternoon, the sun hung low in the sky, bathing the school grounds in a warm golden hue. Most of the events were winding down, the field scattered with tired students and half-deflated enthusiasm. Pearl had been busy all day, darting from one activity to another. I'd barely seen her, except for the occasional wave or hurried exchange of words as she rushed past. It wasn't like her to leave me alone this long, and I couldn't shake the odd pang of loneliness that crept in as I sat by myself under the pavilion.

I t was the most concealed part of the school grounds, a spot where the sounds of cheering and laughter softened into a distant hum. I leaned against one of the wooden beams, letting my gaze drift to the horizon where the light danced against the edge of the field.

I heard the sound of footsteps before I saw him. Brandon.

He came into view with that casual, almost lazy stride of his, but something about him seemed different. His shoulders were slouched, his hands buried deep in his pockets, and his usual smirk was nowhere to be seen. Instead, his expression was soft, almost melancholic, as though the golden light had melted away some unseen armor.

"Didn't expect to find you here," he said, his voice quieter than usual, devoid of its usual edge.

I shrugged, keeping my tone neutral. "Didn't expect you to look for me."

He smirked faintly at that but didn't reply. Instead, he sat down beside me, leaning back against the beam with a heavy sigh.

For a moment, neither of us said anything. The silence stretched, broken only by the distant shouts from the field and the chirping of birds somewhere in the trees.

"Crazy day, huh?" Brandon said eventually, his tone light but with a hint of something deeper.

"Yeah," I replied, not looking at him.

He tilted his head slightly, studying me. "Not your thing, is it? All this running around, getting sweaty for some pointless medal."

I couldn't help but let out a small laugh. "Not exactly."

He chuckled too, a sound that felt oddly genuine. "Me neither."

I turned to look at him then, surprised by the honesty in his voice. Brandon rarely let his guard down like this, especially around me. His eyes were fixed on the horizon, the golden light catching the edges of his face and making him look younger somehow, almost like the boy I remembered from preschool.

"You used to love this kind of stuff," I said, the words slipping out before I could stop them.

He glanced at me, one eyebrow raised. "Did I?"

"Yeah," I said. "Back in preschool. You were always racing around, trying to beat everyone at everything."

He smiled faintly, a wistful look crossing his face. "That was a long time ago."

"It wasn't that long," I said, but the weight in his tone made it clear he felt otherwise.

Brandon let out a soft sigh, his gaze dropping to the ground. "Things were different back then," he said. "Simpler."

I didn't know what to say to that, so I stayed quiet, letting the moment hang between us.

"You remember that time we built that stupid sandcastle?" he asked suddenly, a small smile tugging at the corners of his mouth.

"Which time?" I asked, a little caught off guard.

"The big one," he said, gesturing with his hands as if to illustrate. "The one we spent the whole afternoon on, only for that jerk Robbie to stomp all over it."

I couldn't help but laugh at the memory. "Oh, yeah. You almost tackled him into the sandbox."

"Almost?" Brandon said, his grin widening. "Pretty sure I did."

We both laughed then, the sound easy and unforced, and for a brief moment, it felt like we were kids again, back before everything had gone so wrong.

But the moment didn't last. Brandon's smile faded, replaced by that same melancholic expression he'd worn when he first arrived.

"What happened to us?" he asked, his voice barely above a whisper.

The question caught me off guard, and I didn't know how to answer. There was so much I could have said—about the choices he'd made, the lines he'd crossed—but none of it felt right in that moment.

"I don't know," I said finally, the words feeling inadequate.

Brandon nodded slowly, as if he'd expected that answer. "Neither do I."

The silence returned, heavier this time, and I could feel the weight of unspoken words hanging in the air between us.

"You don't have to keep doing this, you know," I said eventually, my voice hesitant.

"Doing what?" he asked, his tone defensive.

"All of it," I said. "The pills, the groping, the... everything. You don't have to keep being that guy."

He looked at me then, really looked at me, his eyes searching mine for something I couldn't quite name.

"Maybe I do," he said finally, his voice soft but firm. "Maybe that's all I've got left."

I wanted to argue, to tell him he was wrong, but the look on his face stopped me. There was a pain there, a vulnerability he rarely let anyone see, and I realized that no matter what I said, it wouldn't change anything.

The sun was dipping lower now, the golden light fading into shades of orange and pink. Brandon stood up, brushing the dirt off his pants.

"See you around," he said, his tone light but his eyes heavy.

"Yeah," I said, watching as he walked away, his figure silhouetted against the setting sun.

I sat there for a long time after he left, the weight of our conversation pressing down on me. For the first time in years, I saw a glimpse of the boy Brandon used to be, and it made me wonder if there was still a chance for him to find his way back. But as the last rays of sunlight disappeared below the horizon, I couldn't shake the feeling that whatever path Brandon was on, it was one he'd chosen long ago—and one he wasn't ready to leave.

Entry #25
12 March 2012

B randon has reset. Or maybe "reset" isn't the right word—he's snapped back, rebounding into his worst version like a rubber band stretched too tight. It's almost impressive how quickly he's reassembled the pieces of his old self, except now, there's something sharper about him, something more dangerous.

He walks the halls with that swagger again, daring anyone to challenge him. His cocky grin is back in full force, but it's different now—harder, edged with bitterness. His strained relationship with Todd seems to have solidified a colder, meaner persona. Without his usual partner-in-crime to laugh along with him, Brandon's actions seem more deliberate, like he's compensating for the absence of their bond by doubling down on his arrogance.

He doesn't try to hide the changes, either. His appearance practically shouts that something's different. Brandon looks wealthier now, somehow. His clothes are sharp, clean, and expensive-looking—not the usual scuffed-up sneakers and thrift store hoodies he used to wear. His shoes gleam unnaturally, and he's started sporting a gold chain that catches the light whenever he shifts his head.

And the attitude matches the wardrobe. He flaunts it—pulling out wads of cash in the cafeteria, paying for snacks without waiting for change, leaving tips like we're in a fancy restaurant. The other boys stare with barely-concealed envy; the girls, predictably, swoon.

But something about it feels off. None of this suits him. The cocky smile, the new clothes, the cold confidence—it's all a bit too deliberate, like he's wearing a costume and daring us to call him out on it.

I can't help but notice the way people gravitate toward him again, like moths to a flame. He doesn't even need Todd anymore. A new circle has started to form around him—guys who laugh a little too loudly at his jokes, girls who hang off his every word. And he lets them. He's always been a manipulator, but this feels more calculating, more dangerous.

In class, he's unbearable. He interrupts teachers, cracks inappropriate jokes, and smirks whenever he's reprimanded. The teachers sigh and roll their eyes but never truly deal with him. It's like they've given up entirely.

Even Pearl noticed. During lunch, she nudged me and whispered, "He's changed again. But not for the better."

"I don't think he's ever changed for the better," I muttered back, earning a laugh from her.

But deep down, I felt uneasy. His arrogance might be his shield, but the cracks are still there, visible if you know where to look. I caught him staring at Todd during a free period, his expression unreadable. It wasn't anger, exactly. Maybe regret? Or resentment? Whatever it was, it vanished the moment he saw me looking.

Later, in the courtyard, Brandon shoved past me deliberately, knocking my books to the ground.

"Oops," he said with a smirk, bending down to pick up one of my notebooks. But instead of handing it back, he leafed through it like it was his property.

"Nice handwriting," he sneered, tossing it back onto the pile in my arms.

I glared at him, but he just walked away, his laugh echoing as he rejoined his new entourage.

It's exhausting, seeing him like this again. For a moment, after his suspension, I thought he might be different—quieter, subdued. I almost believed that whatever happened during those weeks might have changed him.

But no. Brandon's back, and this time, it feels like he's trying to prove something.

Maybe it's to Todd. Maybe it's to himself. Or maybe it's to all of us.

ENTRY #26

1 June 2012

News of Brandon's latest escapade reached me during lunch—a house party, of course. Not just any house party, but one hosted in the swankiest part of town, in a mansion big enough to swallow our entire school. The buzz among my classmates was electric. Everyone was talking about it, from the jocks to the kids who usually avoided Brandon's orbit.

Everyone but me, it seemed, had received an invitation.

Pearl mentioned it casually, as though it was old news. "You're not going, are you?" she asked, tilting her head.

I blinked. "I didn't even know it was happening."

Her face fell slightly, and I couldn't tell if it was pity or relief. "Oh... well, you're not missing much. Brandon's parties are all noise and nonsense. Trust me."

I nodded, pretending not to care, but the truth was, it stung. Not because I wanted to go—I'd probably be miserable—but because it was another reminder of how far apart Brandon and I had drifted.

He's growing up too fast. That's what hit me as I sat alone later that afternoon, replaying snippets of conversation from the day. Brandon, with his new clothes, new friends, and new attitude, seemed to be sprinting toward some version of adulthood I didn't recognize. A version I didn't want to recognize.

The idea of him hosting a party like this felt surreal. I couldn't imagine him as a host, pouring drinks, turning up the music, laughing with people he probably didn't care about. Yet, that's exactly what he'd do.

And it left me wondering: how will he be in high school? Will he still be this larger-than-life figure, pulling people into his orbit with that dangerous charm? Or will he burn out, crashing under the weight of whatever he's chasing?

I caught myself feeling something close to envy, though not for the reasons you'd expect. It wasn't about the party or the money or the attention. It was about the sheer momentum of his life. Brandon seemed to be speeding toward something—chaotic, yes, but at least it was movement.

And here I was, still stuck in the same place, watching from the sidelines as everyone else moved forward.

ENTRY #27
2 June 2012

Everyone was talking about the party today, and I couldn't help feeling like an outsider looking in. Snatches of conversation floated around the room—who danced with whom, which drinks were strongest, and the inevitable drama that comes with putting teenagers and alcohol together under one roof. Even the teachers seemed to catch some of the buzz, giving us exasperated looks as if we'd collectively lost our focus.

Apparently, Pearl went. She didn't tell me outright, but I caught her hesitating when I asked what she did last night. Her cheeks flushed a little, and she mumbled something about staying up late. I didn't press her. I couldn't blame her for going; if I'd been invited, I probably would've gone too, no matter how much I told myself otherwise.

Not that my gran would've allowed it. The second she'd have heard "Brandon" and "party" in the same sentence, it would've been an immediate no. But the truth was, I didn't even try to ask. My excuse of "studying for the midterms" worked well enough, even though I didn't crack open a single textbook last night.

Instead, I lay in bed, scrolling through my phone, refreshing my social media feed to catch glimpses of the night I was missing. People were tagging Brandon in posts, uploading blurry videos of the party. His house looked like something out of a magazine—sprawling, modern, and way too expensive for someone our age to be living in.

There were rumors Brandon had invited some of his high school friends. They were the ones who supposedly brought the alcohol and the pills. Pink pills, specifically. A "party drug," someone whispered this morning, their eyes wide as if they were recounting a ghost story.

And then there was the artist. A real, actual, *famous* artist, there in Brandon's living room, drinking and laughing as if he were one of us. I don't know how Brandon pulled that off. Actually, I don't know how Brandon pulls off *any* of this.

Where does his money come from? That question keeps circling back in my mind. The mansion, the high-end clothes he's started wearing, the fact that he can throw a party like this without blinking an eye—it doesn't add up.

People like to speculate. Some say his dad must've come into money, though I find that hard to believe given how much of a mess the man always seemed to be. Others think Brandon's got some "side hustle," but what kind of hustle lets a kid live like this?

The jealousy, though—that's what I hate admitting. I was jealous out of my mind last night. Not of the drinking or the dancing or even the artist, but of the way Brandon makes himself the center of the universe. Everyone gravitates toward him, even now. Even after all the horrible things he's done.

How does he do it? That's what I keep asking myself. How does someone like Brandon keep rising, no matter how many times he's been knocked down?

I wonder if this is what high school will be like for him—bigger parties, bigger crowds, and an even bigger divide between the two of us. It's like he's sprinting ahead while I'm still stuck, waiting for life to catch up.

Pearl hasn't brought the party up again, and I'm grateful for it. But I can't shake the feeling that, for her, the night might have been a glimpse of what's coming. For all of us.

The rest of the day passed in a blur of envy and irritation, every laugh or whispered conversation about the party like a pinprick reminder of how far I am from whatever world Brandon lives in now. Maybe it's for the best that I wasn't invited. Maybe the things I'd have seen there would've made me feel even more out of place than I already do.

Still, as I sat in the quiet of my room tonight, staring out the window at the stars, I couldn't help but wonder what it felt like to be there. To be one of them. To live, even for one night, like someone who belongs.

ENTRY #28

4 June 2012

The first Monday after the party, and I don't think I've ever felt smaller.

The morning air buzzed with excitement as people swapped stories from Saturday night. Every conversation seemed to orbit around Brandon's party—how incredible his house was, how wild the night became, how everyone who mattered was there. Everyone except me.

I walked into the classroom, and the noise was overwhelming. Laughter, exaggerated retellings, inside jokes I wasn't privy to. The same people I'd shared lessons and lunches with for years suddenly felt like strangers, part of a club I'd never be allowed to join.

Even Pearl seemed different. She sat with a group of girls near the window, her usually calm demeanor replaced with something... lighter. Happier. I watched as she laughed at something someone said, her face lighting up in a way I hadn't seen in a while. She glanced at me once, and for a fleeting second, I thought she might come over. But she didn't. She just smiled, almost apologetically, and turned back to her conversation.

I shouldn't blame her. It's not her fault I wasn't there.

Brandon walked in a few minutes later, and the room seemed to shift. He was magnetic in a way I can't explain. Confidence radiated from him, an effortless charm that pulled people closer even as he sauntered past without acknowledging them. He looked more polished than usual, like he'd spent the entire weekend bathing in compliments and soaking up the admiration of everyone who'd attended.

I kept my head down, hoping he wouldn't notice me. But part of me also wished he would.

What would he even say? Probably nothing. Probably something sharp and cutting, just to remind me of my place.

The conversations didn't die down for the rest of the day. Even in the classes where the teachers tried to keep us focused, whispers still made their way around the room. People talked about the expensive liquor Brandon had, the pool that glittered like something out of a movie, the music so loud it vibrated through the walls.

And then there were the rumors.

Apparently, Brandon's "high school friends" brought more than just alcohol. Someone said they saw him slip something to one of the older girls, the same pink pills I'd heard about before. Others mentioned seeing him in the backyard, too close to someone for comfort. The stories felt larger than life, but they carried a dark edge.

How does someone like Brandon even have access to that kind of world? It doesn't make sense, not when you think about it. Or maybe it does, and I'm just too naive to see it.

I couldn't concentrate all day. It felt like I was standing at the edge of something huge, something I couldn't fully understand but knew was dangerous. And yet, everyone else seemed fine with it. Excited, even.

By the time the final bell rang, I felt like I'd been holding my breath for hours. As I walked home, the conversations from school replayed in my mind, louder than the traffic on the street.

Brandon is growing up too fast. That's the thought I can't shake. He's sprinting ahead into a life I can't keep up with, a life I'm not even sure he's ready for.

What will he be like in high school? That's the question that keeps circling in my mind. Will he get worse? Or will something—someone—finally stop him?

And where does that leave me? Still on the sidelines, watching everything unfold from a distance, wondering if I'll ever be part of the story.

Entry #29
25 June 2012

Midterm week—a necessary evil that brings the entire school into an anxious frenzy. The classroom felt like a pressure cooker today, with students hunched over their notes, frantically cramming in the minutes before exams started. For most of us, this week is a battleground. For Brandon, it's just another stage to dominate.

It's hard not to notice the quiet assembly line of girls orbiting him. They linger around his desk between exams, holding folded notes like offerings, their faces a strange mix of nervousness and eagerness. Some of the notes are instructions for him, while others—judging by the sly smiles and whispers—seem far more personal.

Then there are the assignments. I watched in disbelief as girls slid neatly written essays and homework pages onto his desk, whispering assurances that everything was done just as he wanted. I wonder if they're hoping for a sliver of his attention or if this is his currency—a power dynamic he has mastered.

Brandon, of course, thrives on it. He lounges at his desk like a king holding court, barely glancing at the girls or their offerings. He knows they'll keep coming back, and they do. It's infuriating, really. Not just the control he exerts, but the way he wears it so easily, as though the world owes him this deference.

It's not just the girls in our class, either. I caught glimpses of students from other grades stopping by, their faces painted with the same eager deference. Brandon barely acknowledges them, sometimes flashing a half-smile or tossing a sarcastic remark, but it's enough to keep them hooked.

I find myself wondering what they see in him. Is it the charisma? The confidence? Or is it something darker, the allure of someone who always seems untouchable? Whatever it is, it feeds into the vortex of control he seems to wield over anyone who comes too close.

It's hard to focus on exams with all this playing out around me. While the rest of us are panicking over formulas and essay prompts, Brandon doesn't even pretend to care. He leans back in his chair, flipping through someone else's notes, or smirking at the chaos around him.

Pearl mentioned it briefly during lunch. She tried to brush it off, but I could see the unease in her expression. "It's ridiculous," she said, stabbing at her sandwich with a plastic fork. "They're just feeding his ego."

I wanted to agree, but there was something in her voice—something that made me wonder if she felt as powerless as I did to stop it.

Brandon's control isn't just confined to academics or these desperate gestures of admiration. It's in the way he moves through the hallways, the way teachers hesitate to reprimand him, the way even the most popular boys seem to defer to him. It's like he's created his own rules, and no one dares to challenge them.

By the end of the day, my frustration has settled into a dull ache. It's not just jealousy, though I'd be lying if I said that wasn't part of it. It's the helplessness of watching someone like Brandon bend the world to his will while the rest of us scramble to keep up.

As I walk home, my mind is crowded with thoughts of the exams, the girls, and that unshakable sense of imbalance. Brandon may be king for now, but kings don't reign forever.

ENTRY #30
17 September 2012

I don't know when it started—this silence between me and Pearl. I couldn't pinpoint the exact day it became a gap that couldn't be bridged. At first, it was just the usual busyness of school, the need to focus on the constant stream of assignments and exams. But as the days turned into weeks, I started to notice the absence. I texted her a few times, but my messages were left unanswered. Even at school, she wasn't there—her seat empty, her laughter a ghost in the back of my mind.

I didn't think much of it at first. She'd always been unpredictable, in a way. Maybe she was just busy, or maybe she was going through something. She'd always had her secrets, just like the rest of us.

But today, as I stepped off the bus and made my way towards the school entrance, something felt off. The air was thick with a tension I couldn't place, and as I walked past groups of students huddled in small clusters, I noticed the hushed voices and the tear-streaked faces. People were crying. Eyes were red, pupils wide with shock. There was an undeniable weight in the atmosphere, a kind of sorrow that seemed to seep into every corner of the school.

I tried to ignore it at first, chalking it up to some drama or another. But the closer I got to the homeroom, the heavier the air became. It wasn't just sadness—it was something else, something darker.

When I entered the classroom, I was met by the somber silence of the room. The teacher, Mrs. Lancaster, stood at the front, her back turned to the class as if she had been waiting for me. Her shoulders were hunched, her head slightly lowered, and when she finally turned to face me, her face was pale, stricken with grief.

She saw me, and for a brief moment, it was as if she hadn't recognized me at all. I stood still by the door, unsure of what was happening. The students around me were staring at their desks, some with their hands over their faces, others with eyes wide and unblinking.

Mrs. Lancaster didn't move right away, just slowly crossed the room to where I stood. Her steps were heavy, deliberate. When she reached me, she placed a hand on my shoulder, her voice breaking the stillness. "I'm so sorry," she whispered.

The words didn't register at first. My mind struggled to catch up with the reality of the situation, but Mrs. Lancaster, sensing my confusion, stepped closer and spoke again.

"Pearl is gone," she said, her voice shaking. "She was found... she was found this morning. There was an assault, and..." Her words trailed off as if the weight of them was too much for her to bear.

I stared at her, unblinking, unable to comprehend what I was hearing. Pearl? My friend? Gone? How?

"There's been a terrible tragedy," Mrs. Lancaster continued, her eyes darting toward the other students in the room. "It wasn't just an accident. It was... deliberate." Her voice broke again, and I could feel the tears welling up in her eyes as she struggled to keep composure.

I shook my head, refusing to believe it. Pearl couldn't be dead. Not Pearl, not now, not like this. We were just talking a few weeks ago. How could she be gone? And how could this have happened?

"They found her... they found her body near the outskirts of town, behind an old abandoned building," Mrs. Lancaster said, her words coming out in rushed, fragmented bursts. "There was no mistake. She was... she was assaulted, and then left there. The police are still investigating."

The room around me blurred into the background, and I couldn't hear anything else. All I could think about was Pearl. The last time I saw her—just days ago, laughing, as carefree as ever. The thought that something like this could happen to someone so close to me felt like a punch to the stomach. It didn't seem real.

How could anyone do something like that? How could they hurt her?

Mrs. Lancaster's voice barely cut through the fog in my head. "I know this is a lot to process. I'm so sorry. I know you were close to her." She paused, then added softly, "You're not alone in this. We'll get through it together."

But I wasn't sure how I was supposed to process it, how to make sense of the fact that someone had taken Pearl from us so violently, so senselessly. She was my friend, my classmate. We weren't supposed to lose people like that. Not like this.

As I stood there, my legs feeling like lead, I couldn't stop thinking about the cruel irony of it all. Pearl had been so full of life, so unafraid to be herself in a world that tried to crush people like her. She was unapologetic, confident in ways I could never be. But now she was gone, and all I could feel was the weight of the silence she left behind.

The bell rang, signaling the start of the next class, but I didn't hear it. I didn't even register the movement around me. My mind kept replaying Mrs. Lancaster's words, over and over. Pearl had been taken—violated—and I couldn't wrap my mind around it.

Somehow, I ended up outside, walking aimlessly, not sure where I was going. My head was spinning, my thoughts fragmented. The school was still buzzing with hushed whispers and sideways glances, but I felt detached from it all. None of it mattered. Pearl was gone. Nothing else could compare to that.

As I walked, I wondered what kind of world we were living in. How could anyone hurt another person like that? How could someone do that to someone so kind, so full of potential? I thought about everything we'd shared, the way she had always been there for me—even when I didn't deserve it. And now she was gone, and I hadn't even been there when she needed someone the most.

I don't know how long I walked, but when I finally came to my senses, I found myself by the edge of town, staring at the old building where they had found Pearl. It looked abandoned, derelict, just like the rest of the world seemed now. The sun had set, and the air was cool, but I couldn't move. I just stood there, staring at the place where she'd been taken from us.

The silence was deafening.

ENTRY #31
2 January 2013
High School Orientation Day

The air in the gymnasium is thick with excitement and unease. The seniors are standing at the front in their neat uniforms, their confident postures commanding attention. I try not to stare, but it's impossible to ignore them. They carry themselves with a sort of authority that makes everything feel... small.

Brandon, of course, is among them, slipping into his role as the popular senior with ease. His confidence is now on another level—too polished for my liking. But there's something about him that draws people in, even when they seem wary of him. And it's not just me—everyone in the room notices him.

But there are others too—seniors I haven't met, but who are already asserting themselves in ways that seem both natural and imposing. They laugh among themselves, talk, and move like they've been here forever. It's hard not to feel like an outsider, watching them as they interact like they're part of something bigger, something I'll never be.

I look around at the seniors, each one standing out in their own way. The room seems to pulse with their different energies, their auras mixing together and filling the space with a kind of quiet chaos.

1. **Caden** – With messy brown hair falling over his forehead, Caden exudes a laid-back confidence. His green eyes glint mischievously as he watches the room, and though he has an almost lazy demeanor, you can tell there's a sharp mind underneath that carefree attitude. He's always got something witty to say, and it's no surprise that his chuckles are contagious. People are drawn to him, and his sense of humor gives him an edge.

2. **Selene** – She stands beside Caden, small but commanding. Selene has long, raven-black hair that cascades in waves, and her eyes are sharp, constantly scanning the room. There's something almost intimidating about her—not in a mean way, but in the way she can dissect everything around her in an instant. When she speaks, it's with quiet authority, and you can't help but listen.

3. **Archer** – Archer is built like a linebacker—tall and muscular, with broad shoulders that make him look like he could crush anyone who challenged him. His buzzed hair and stoic demeanor give him a serious air, but when he speaks, it's with a quiet intensity. He's the type who doesn't waste words, and though he doesn't say much, when he does, everyone stops to listen. People respect him without needing to try.

4. **Juno** – Juno is a whirlwind of energy, small in stature but larger than life. With bouncy, golden curls and a

laugh that fills any room, she's impossible to ignore. She wears bright colors, her attire always an eccentric mix of patterns and textures that make her stand out. Juno's energy is infectious, and even if she talks too fast, you can't help but follow her along, swept up in her constant enthusiasm.

5. **Ronan** – Ronan is one of the quieter seniors, with dark brown hair and a brooding presence that makes people keep their distance. He's tall and thin, folding himself into himself like he's constantly retreating into his own world. His dark eyes miss nothing, always watching, always calculating. When he speaks, it's with a deep, thoughtful tone, but his words feel heavy—like he's holding something back.

6. **Nova** – Nova is the eccentric one, the type of person who doesn't quite fit any mold. She wears oversized jackets, large round glasses, and sports brightly colored sneakers. She's loud, animated, and always gesturing wildly as she talks. Nova is the kind of person you either love or hate, but no one can deny that she draws attention without even trying. She's a force of nature, and everyone around her can't help but be swept into her orbit.

7. **Kieran** – Kieran has this natural, almost aristocratic elegance to him. With perfectly styled platinum blonde hair and immaculate skin, he's the kind of person who seems like they've stepped out of a magazine cover. He walks with a grace that's almost too practiced, and when he speaks, people listen—because they know he's not one to waste his

words. There's something deeply calculated about him, but it's wrapped in a smooth, charming exterior.

8. **Dashiell** – Dashiell stands off to the side, quietly observing. His shaggy hair frames his face, and his dark, intense eyes seem to take everything in without letting anyone see what's behind them. He's the type of person who blends into the background, but when he speaks, it's like the whole room goes silent. He doesn't need to shout for attention—he commands it with his presence alone.

9. **Eris** – With her fiery red hair and exuberant energy, Eris is impossible to miss. She's short, but the way she carries herself makes her seem bigger. She's always laughing, always making jokes, and people gravitate toward her even when they're not quite sure why. Eris has a knack for lighting up any room, and her passion for whatever she's doing is palpable. Even when she's exhausted, she still somehow manages to keep the energy high.

10. **Dorian** – Dorian is the athlete—the guy everyone knows will be the star of whatever sports team he joins. He's tall, broad-shouldered, and built like a tank, with short, messy hair and a perpetual smirk. There's something about him that makes people both admire and fear him. His smile is as sharp as his physique, and when he talks, his voice is confident and self-assured. He doesn't need to prove anything to anyone—but he enjoys showing off anyway.

As I watch them, I feel a pang of loneliness, realizing just how out of place I am. I don't know how I'll fit in with these people—how I'll ever be anything more than just a passive observer in their world. They're already a part of something I can't reach, a group that's light years ahead of me in every way. And then my mind comes back to Brandon—how easily he slides into this role, how everyone around him follows his lead without question.

But I'm not one of them.

I'm just... me. And high school, from what I can see, isn't built for someone like me.

The seniors start to disperse, and I can't shake the feeling that I've just witnessed something monumental. This isn't just the start of a school year. This is the beginning of everything. And I'm not sure where I belong in it all.

ENTRY #32
8 January 2013

The first week of high school has felt like an endless blur—packed with rehearsals for the Junior Induction play that have kept us all busy late into the night. Everyone is scrambling to memorize lines, prepare costumes, and fake excitement about what's supposed to be some grand, life-changing moment. I'm sure it means more to the upperclassmen, but to us juniors? It's just another task, another thing to check off the list.

Brandon and I are in different classes now, each of us with our own kind of people. He ended up with a rowdy crew, people who barely seem to care about anything except the next prank or fight, people who make noise for the sake of making noise. They're the type who find enjoyment in chaos, who drag each other down into the mess of high school's underbelly without hesitation. Honestly, I'm not surprised. It's a group that suits him. He blends in so effortlessly that it's almost too easy to forget there was a time when he was someone different, someone I used to know in a way that seems so distant now.

Then there's me—stuck in a class with what I can only describe as the "better" crowd. They're smart, refined, polite almost to the point of being intimidating. It's not that I don't like them, but it's like they live in a different world, one where everything is neatly planned, where nothing seems to ever go wrong. There's an undercurrent of pressure, an invisible expectation to rise to a certain standard, and I'm still grappling with how I'm supposed to fit in. I don't want to be that person who tries too hard, but I don't want to be invisible either. So, for now, I'm the guy who keeps his head down and stays in the middle of it all—avoiding notice, but still trying to make it through.

Ms. Megan, our homeroom teacher, has become this unexpected force in my school life. I used to think teachers were either tough or kind, black-and-white in their personalities, but Ms. Megan is different. She's got this energy about her that doesn't scream authority but still demands it, like she's earned the right to have everyone listen. Tall with dark curly hair, she's got a presence that fills the room without her even trying. I noticed how she holds her gaze—never too soft, but never too harsh either. There's a knowing look in her eyes, like she's seen enough to understand when someone is bullshitting and when they're telling the truth.

I can't help but feel like she's got me figured out. Her silence sometimes speaks louder than her words. I can tell when she's watching me—no judgment, just observation. She doesn't rush to speak but when she does, it's always on point, cutting straight to whatever matters. There's no pretending in her class. She sees through all of it, and I get the feeling she's waiting for me to show her who I really am.

I think that's what keeps me on edge, this feeling that I need to rise to something, to prove something not just to the class but to myself. It's an uncomfortable realization—that high school isn't a fresh start like I hoped, but a place where expectations are higher and harder to escape from. There's nowhere to hide now, no running away from the things I tried to bury.

And then there's Brandon—always on my mind, even though I try not to think about him too much. I wonder if he's feeling the pressure of all this. I can't tell if he even cares. Every day he walks through the halls like he's already on top of the world, making people laugh, causing trouble, and keeping his distance from anything that requires him to be serious. It's as if he's chosen to stay the same, to be that person who never changes no matter how many years go by. I wonder how long he can keep it up, though. High school is different. It's not the same as middle school. I don't think anyone really gets it until they're in it, but the moment you step in, the rules change.

I don't know if I'll ever be able to talk to him again the way I used to. There's this chasm between us now, one that grows wider every time I see him joking around with the same group of kids who make the world feel smaller and smaller. He doesn't need me anymore, I guess. He's got his group. And I've got mine—or, at least, I'll figure it out.

Ms. Megan finally stands up to start the lesson, and I try to shake off all these thoughts swirling in my head. High school has barely started, and I already feel like I'm drowning in everything. But for now, I'll play it cool. I'll do what I need to do, keep my head down, and try to make it through another day. Just one day at a time. That's all I can do.

ENTRY #33
28 January 2013

Everything has been going smoothly lately. My classmates are all refined, friendly, and genuinely pleasant to be around. There's a real sense of camaraderie in the air, and I've been starting to feel like I belong here. The rehearsals for the upcoming concert on the 4th of February have been enjoyable. We're all working together, and it feels like progress. There's this quiet excitement building as the performance date approaches, and even though I'm not the star of the show, I feel connected to something bigger than myself for once.

It's strange, really. I thought high school would be different, like everything would be more isolating or overwhelming. But so far, it hasn't been. I've made a few connections, and there's a sense of peace I didn't expect to find. Maybe it's because I'm finally in a class where people want to succeed and be good to one another. I can't say I've formed any real close friendships yet, but I'm comfortable. I'm not on the outside looking in, as I once feared I would be.

The concert is coming up fast, and there's a lot of prep to do, but I'm finding the process fun rather than stressful. I'm not used to that feeling—usually, the pressure of something like this would've had me second-guessing everything, but this time, it's different. It feels natural. Maybe this is what high school is supposed to be like—challenging, sure, but manageable when you're surrounded by the right people. The right environment.

Brandon, on the other hand, seems to be coasting. He's doing his thing, being his usual charismatic self, but he's not someone I've been hanging around with much lately. Honestly, I haven't seen much of him. Not that I'm complaining, but it's strange. He's still in my peripheral vision, of course—he's everywhere—but he's becoming a figure I don't know how to approach anymore. Maybe that's a good thing. Maybe it's better to just focus on this new chapter and leave the past behind. We'll see how things unfold from here.

For now, I'll enjoy this small, peaceful moment. Everything seems to be in place, and I'm content with where things are going.

ENTRY #34
5 February 2013

I spoke too soon. I should have known things wouldn't stay perfect for long. The concert was a success, and I was proud to win the Best Supporting Actor trophy. But now? Now, it feels like I've been hit with a tidal wave.

Someone—somehow—let it slip that I'm gay. It wasn't supposed to get out. At least, not like this. I'm sure it was Brandon. He was always good at planting seeds and watching them grow into something far worse. I can almost hear his voice now, the way he'd casually slip something into conversation, always with that smirk of his, like he knew exactly what would come of it. Like he knew how easy it would be to make me the punchline of his little joke.

And now, it's spreading. I'm getting the sideways glances, the uncomfortable silences, and the whispers behind my back. People don't look at me the same anymore, and it's suffocating. It's not just the boys—it's the girls too. They look at me like I'm some kind of puzzle they can't figure out. And the pity... I can see it in their eyes, masked by forced smiles.

I've tried to pretend it doesn't bother me. I've even tried to convince myself that it doesn't matter. But it does. I can feel it in every conversation I have now. It's like this invisible wall has been put up between me and everyone else. Like the mask I wore to blend in has cracked, and now they can see me for what I am. Or at least, what they think I am.

I can't stop thinking about Brandon. How he must be enjoying this, laughing to himself at how easily he manipulated things. It's always been a game to him—he enjoys playing with people, testing their limits. I wouldn't put it past him to be the one who let the truth slip, just to watch the chaos unfold.

But it's not just the gossip that hurts. It's the feeling of being exposed, like a secret has been ripped away from me. I wasn't ready for this. I didn't want it out in the open.

I don't know how I'm going to get through this. I want to pretend that none of it matters, that people will forget, that things will go back to normal. But I can't shake the feeling that they won't. Things have changed. They've changed, and I'm not sure I can ever go back.

ENTRY #35
1 March 2013

I should have known it was coming. I should have seen the way their eyes lingered on me, the subtle shifts in their movements as they positioned themselves around me. But I didn't. I was too busy thinking about how I could get through the day, trying to ignore the weight of the whispers and the looks.

But they weren't going to let me off that easy.

I didn't expect it to happen like this. It wasn't a fight. Not really. It was just... a beating. The kind where the air around you gets thicker, and your brain starts to fog up. The first punch came out of nowhere. My stomach twisted in a way that had nothing to do with pain. I hadn't even seen who it was. It didn't matter. They didn't want a fight; they just wanted me to know my place.

The rest of them joined in quickly, taking turns in some twisted rhythm. My body went into autopilot—moving, reacting, but not really feeling. I couldn't even remember how long it lasted. Minutes? Hours?

I remember the dizziness. My head swam, and I could taste the blood, but there was no anger. It wasn't like the fights I'd had with myself in my head—those were battles I could fight.

This wasn't a battle. This was just me being reminded of how little I mattered to them.

And that was the real wound.

When they finally stopped, when their laughter died down and they all backed off, I didn't rise. I didn't try to get up. I just sat there for a moment, on the ground, feeling the world around me spin and settle. Something inside me felt... different. Something inside me changed.

I didn't feel defeated. I didn't feel weak. I didn't even feel the rage I expected. Instead, I felt cold. A strange, empty kind of calm that settled into my chest. I realized I had expected too much from people. I had thought that maybe, just maybe, there was a chance I could get through all this without being broken. But that was before. This was after.

And after? After, I understood the rules better.

It was clear now. They weren't going to stop. They were never going to stop. And maybe, just maybe, they were right about one thing. Maybe I *wasn't* worth their time to care about. They could laugh at me. They could beat me down. But I wasn't going to give them the satisfaction of seeing me crumble.

I wasn't going to give anyone the satisfaction of seeing me break.

I stood up slowly, feeling the bruises start to form, the cuts on my lips stinging. I wiped the blood from my mouth with the back of my hand and took a long breath. There was a fire inside me now—faint, but it was there. Not a fire to fight back, not in the way they expected, but a fire to protect what was left of me. To keep the last shred of myself hidden, like a flame tucked deep inside where they couldn't reach it.

But they thought they had me figured out. They thought I was just some weak kid they could push around. They thought I would cower.

And then there was Brandon. I didn't know what was worse—what they did to me or the fact that I saw his face in the crowd of boys who stood around me. He didn't lay a hand on me, but I could see the smile on his face, the satisfaction in his eyes as he watched it happen. I couldn't help but think, *this was him*, in some way. The seed of all this. I thought maybe he would've grown up by now, maybe he'd changed, but there was that same glint in his eyes. He was still the same person. Only now, he wasn't just tormenting me. He was enjoying it.

But I wouldn't let him win this time. He thought he could break me. Well, he couldn't.

I've learned something important today. I've learned that it doesn't matter how many bruises they leave, or how many times they hit you. The real fight happens when you stop caring about what they think, when you stop letting them get inside your head. The real fight is when you learn to be something else, something better, something they can never break.

And that's the fight I'm going to win. Because this time, I won't let them see my defeat. This time, I'll rise differently.

They can throw everything at me, but they won't get the satisfaction of seeing me break.

Not again.

And the weirdest part of all? I didn't feel sorry for myself. Not at all. I felt... free. For the first time in a long time, I felt free. The game had changed, and I was no longer playing by their rules.

I'm playing by mine now.

It's a new chapter.

ENTRY #36
11 March 2013

I've been thinking a lot about Pearl lately. It's strange, how someone can be here one moment and gone the next. Her absence feels... heavy. But it's not just the fact that she's dead that bothers me. It's that she's no longer here to shield me, to act as some sort of barrier between me and everything that's wrong with this place. She was the only one who ever seemed to care, even if it was in her own flawed way.

The truth is, even before her death, I felt betrayed by her. She pulled away, not just from me, but from everything—her detachment in the last few months, her silence when I needed her most. It wasn't overt, but it was there. She didn't speak up when she should have. She didn't defend me when Brandon and the others turned on me. She just... faded. Maybe she thought I could handle it on my own. Or maybe she was too busy with her own mess. Either way, I've been left to deal with the fallout alone.

I can't ignore it anymore. It's starting to feel like she wasn't the person I thought she was. She was just another girl—another one of those naive, self-centered people who get swept up in the drama of it all, only to disappear when the storm hits.

And now I see it more clearly than I ever have before: the girls at school are no better than the boys. They're all just pieces on a board, playing the same game. They may smile and act like they care, but when push comes to shove, they'll step back and let you take the fall.

I know it's wrong to feel this way, but it's hard not to when the only person who ever stood by me is gone, and the rest are just... there. I think I'm starting to hate them, in a way. Maybe I'm being too harsh. Maybe it's just the pain talking. But whatever it is, it's making me feel bitter.

I've decided I can't keep letting people walk over me. I'm done with being passive, done with waiting for someone else to fix things. I've been playing the victim for too long. It's time to flip the script. If I'm going to survive here, I need to stop running from the truth. The truth is, Brandon's been pulling the strings from the shadows, and I've let him do it.

But no more. I'm taking control.

I'm calling a meeting with him tomorrow. Just the two of us. There's a lot I want to say, a lot I need to get off my chest. And if I have to make him listen, then so be it. The tables have turned, and I'm done being passive.

This might be my last chance to make him see who's really in charge. It might be the beginning of something else entirely. Either way, I'm not backing down.

The game has changed.

INTERLUDE

A s I sit across from Brandon, the silence between us thick with unspoken tension. The recorder clicks on, and I take a deep breath, trying to steady myself before diving into the next question.

"So, do you remember what we talked about on March 12th? That conversation?" I ask, my tone measured but curious, hoping to see some flicker of recognition in his eyes.

Brandon smirks, leaning back in his chair, his expression dripping with that all-too-familiar arrogance. "No," he replies with a condescending chuckle, "How could I remember such a specific day?"

His dismissal stings, but I'm not surprised. I expected nothing less from him. He doesn't even seem to care about the history we shared, the words we exchanged. To him, it's all just noise now—insignificant and unimportant.

The room feels colder now, the air thick with a sense of finality. I'm tempted to ask more, to push harder, but instead, I change the subject. There's no point in dwelling on the past. Not anymore.

I turn the recorder off, the click echoing in the quiet room, before moving on to the next question. It's time to focus on the present—the here and now. And yet, even as I shift the conversation, I can't help but feel a nagging sense that something crucial was left unsaid, a thread left dangling that I'll never be able to pull.

With the shift in focus, we begin to talk again, but something in me knows this isn't the end of our story. Not by a long shot. And maybe, just maybe, there's more to uncover about Brandon, about what's really driving him. I'm not done yet.

ENTRY #37
12 March 2013

I've never been one for confrontation. I've avoided it, let it slide, and hoped that time would take care of things. But today, I had had enough. The buildup over the past few months had festered—Brandon's smug face, his power, the way he treated people like they were beneath him, disposable. I couldn't take it anymore. I couldn't keep pretending I wasn't watching him destroy everyone in his wake. And today, I was going to make him confront it, confront *me*.

I found him by the lockers. He was as usual: aloof, leaning against the cold metal with his hands stuffed in his hoodie pockets, looking at nothing in particular. But I knew better. His eyes were always searching for someone to control, someone to break, someone to manipulate. And I was done being his pawn.

"You've been avoiding me," he said, not even looking up. It wasn't a question, more of an observation, but I could feel the condescension dripping from his words. It always felt like I was beneath him, like I always would be.

"I've been watching you, Brandon," I said, my voice steady but laced with the years of pent-up frustration. I took a step closer, the air between us thick with something unspoken. "And I've seen how you treat people. You can't even survive without a crony to back you up, can you? You've always needed someone to prop up your pathetic existence."

Brandon scoffed, a smirk tugging at his lips as if I had just told him a bad joke. "Really? That's what you think?" His eyes finally met mine, and I could see the challenge in them. He wasn't used to being confronted like this. He was used to being the one with all the answers. "You think I need anyone?"

"You don't need anyone, you just control them," I replied, my voice sharp, the words cutting deeper than I intended. "You get them to do your bidding, write your notes, do your homework. You know the ones I'm talking about, all those girls who follow you around like they're desperate for approval. But you don't care about them. You just use them. You *always* use people."

Brandon's expression faltered for the briefest moment. I could see it in his eyes—he wasn't used to being caught off guard. But it quickly morphed into a sneer, his shoulders stiffening as he leaned into the tension. "You don't know anything about me," he said quietly, though I could hear the rage in his voice, bubbling just beneath the surface.

"Oh, but I do," I continued, not backing down. "I see everything, Brandon. The way you treat people like toys. And I see how you hide behind your 'power.' You can't even stand being around your dad, can you? You're a coward when he's around. You think you can just hide your insecurities by acting tough, but we all see through you."

His face twisted in something between anger and disbelief. "Don't talk about my father," he spat. "You don't know shit about him. About *me*." His jaw clenched, and I knew that if I pushed him too far, things would escalate. But I couldn't stop.

"I'm just asking, Brandon," I said, the words slipping out before I could stop myself. "Where's your sister gone? Or did she finally figure out what kind of man you are and decide she was better off as a prostitute somewhere?"

The shift in Brandon's demeanor was instant, violent. His eyes darkened, narrowing to slits. His breathing became heavy, ragged. His fists clenched, his knuckles white. I knew I had crossed a line. But it didn't matter. This was the moment.

"You don't talk about her," he growled, his voice low and threatening, the words leaving a chill in the air. "You don't *ever* talk about her. You don't know anything about her."

I stood my ground, though my heart raced in my chest. I wasn't afraid anymore. Not of him. "I'm just asking. Where did she go? Or was she just another one of your *broken toys*?"

And just like that, everything snapped. Without warning, Brandon's fist was in my stomach, knocking the breath out of me. I staggered back, gasping, but I didn't fall. I had expected something—just not this fast. The pain was sharp, but I didn't show it.

Brandon came at me again, grabbing me by the collar and slamming me against the locker. His face was inches from mine, his breath hot against my skin. "You're going to regret that," he said, his voice filled with venom. "You don't know what you're talking about."

I pushed against him, trying to break free, but my body felt weak from the punch. "I'm not afraid of you," I whispered, though I could feel the fear creeping in. He was angry, too angry, and I couldn't predict what he would do next.

For a moment, he just stood there, staring at me, as if he was trying to decide what to do. Then, without another word, he shoved me away, stepping back with a grim expression on his face. He ran a hand through his hair, exhaling sharply as if trying to calm himself down.

"You're pathetic," he muttered, his voice quieter now, almost distant. "You think you can just talk to me like that and nothing will happen? You don't know anything about me."

I stood there, staring at him, trying to steady my breath, my heart still pounding in my chest. He had snapped. He was no longer the untouchable Brandon I had once feared. He was just another scared, broken kid who didn't know how to deal with his own demons.

"I don't need to know," I said, my voice cold. "I just know that you're a coward, and you always will be."

Brandon didn't respond. He didn't even look back. He just turned and walked away, leaving me standing there, still reeling from the encounter.

As I stood there, clutching my side where he had hit me, I realized something. Something had changed in me today. I wasn't afraid of him anymore. I didn't need to be. And maybe, just maybe, I had finally broken through that wall he had spent so long building around himself. He wasn't invincible. He wasn't untouchable. He was just another person hiding behind a mask, pretending to be something he wasn't.

And that, for once, felt like victory.

ENTRY #38
16 APRIL 2013

The more I watch Brandon, the clearer it becomes how deep his spiral goes. His behavior has become increasingly erratic, not just with the boys he associates with, but with the girls too. I can't ignore the whispers circulating around him—there are too many rumors now, all centered on his treatment of girls. Girls who were once eager to be around him now avoid his gaze. I overhear conversations where people refer to him as a "sexual assaulter," and though no one ever directly accuses him, it's hard to ignore the way he flaunts his conquests.

He's always been the kind of guy who uses his charm and his good looks to get what he wants, but it's different now. It's no longer about flirting or playing the game—he's become brazen in his approach. His eyes are more calculating, his words more forceful. He no longer has to beg or seduce—he takes. And it's unsettling.

I don't know what it is that drives him now, whether it's a desire for power, control, or just pure emptiness. But I see it, I can feel it—the way he's willing to hurt people just to feel something. There's a cruelty in his actions, a coldness that wasn't there before. He's more reckless now too. I've seen him grab at girls in hallways, pulling them into corners, his hands roaming as if he owns them. And what's worse is the look on his face—like he's daring anyone to stop him.

At times, I think about stepping in. Maybe pulling a teacher aside, saying something. But then I think back to the person Brandon has become and I know it wouldn't matter. He's untouchable in his world. He's learned how to manipulate the people around him, how to control them with his words, his presence. Teachers turn a blind eye when they think it's just "Brandon being Brandon." His popularity, his ability to make people laugh and feel good about themselves, it shields him. He's got them all fooled.

But I'm not fooled. I see what he's becoming. And it's frightening.

When he first started acting out—getting into fights, lashing out in school—there was a part of me that thought it was just a phase. A cry for attention, maybe, or a response to whatever was going on at home. But now I see it for what it is: a part of who he is, a deep-rooted part of his psyche that has twisted him into something darker. Something monstrous.

But it's not just the girls that Brandon has begun to dominate; it's everyone around him. I've watched him tear people apart without a second thought. It's like there's nothing left of the kid I once knew. I can't remember the last time he showed any real kindness, any hint of remorse for anything he's done. He's turned into someone who feeds off the pain of others, someone who thrives on destruction.

I remember the first time he made a girl cry. It was during a break, just before lunch. She was a freshman, one of the quieter ones who didn't get involved in the drama of school. Brandon had cornered her by the lockers, his back pressed to the wall as he loomed over her. I didn't hear their conversation, but I saw the look in her eyes as she tried to back away from him. And I saw the way he smirked, leaning in closer. When she finally walked away, her face was flushed with embarrassment, her eyes glassy with tears. I could hear her friends whispering in the halls later, the rumors flying fast.

It wasn't just that moment, though. It's the accumulation of them. The way Brandon would touch girls at parties, brushing against them with a knowing grin. The way he would force them to laugh at his jokes, or pressure them into doing things they didn't want to do. It's like he has no regard for anyone except himself, like he sees other people as tools to be used.

The worst part? He's good at it. Too good. He knows exactly what to say to get people to do what he wants, and when they don't, he punishes them. He's started isolating certain people, using his influence to tear apart friendships, to pit people against each other for his own amusement. He's become a puppeteer, controlling everyone around him with subtle manipulations and threats.

I can't even tell anyone. Who would believe me? Who would believe the quiet kid who's always been there, watching from the sidelines? Even now, as I write this, I feel like I'm losing my mind. No one else seems to see it, or if they do, they don't care. It's like he's an untouchable king, ruling over all of us from his throne of manipulation and cruelty.

There's no denying it now—Brandon is becoming something darker. The way he speaks about his family, the way he talks about girls, the way he looks at the world—it all screams power. He's obsessed with it, and he's willing to do anything to maintain control. His arrogance has grown. He no longer hides behind jokes or charm; he's openly hostile now. He's no longer the charming, reckless boy I once knew—he's a predator. A bully. A monster.

I keep hearing whispers about how Brandon is "getting help," but I don't believe it. How can he be helped when he doesn't want to change? The way he isolates himself, the way he walks around like he's untouchable—he's built a wall around himself, and he's too deep inside it to even see how far he's fallen.

I don't know if I should try to reach out to him, try to talk to him like I once would. But something tells me it's too late for that. He's beyond reach now. He's beyond saving.

There are days when I think I should say something. Tell someone. But what would I say? How do you explain to someone that the boy you once called a friend is becoming a monster? How do you even begin to make sense of something like that?

I'm left to watch, to observe, as Brandon digs his hole deeper. I wonder how much longer he can keep this up, how much longer he can get away with this. And I wonder—when he finally crashes and burns, when the mask finally slips and everyone sees him for what he is—will I be the one left to pick up the pieces?

Or will I have been too scared to do anything at all?

The more I think about it, the more I realize that I've been watching this whole time. Watching him destroy everyone around him, watching him fall further and further, all while pretending not to notice. But I've seen the signs. I've seen the way he's pushed everyone away, how he's made it clear that he's in control and no one can touch him. He's untouchable. At least, for now.

And then I think about the girls—how many of them are going to be left broken in his wake? How many more will he hurt before someone finally sees him for what he is?

There's no turning back for Brandon now. He's already crossed the line. And as much as I wish I could go back to the days when we were friends, I know it's too late. The person who sits across from me now is not the same boy who once made me laugh, who once shared secrets with me. The boy I knew is gone, replaced by a monster who cares for nothing but power.

I can only watch from the sidelines as Brandon continues to burn everything around him to the ground. And I wonder, as I sit here, writing this—what will be left when it all falls apart? What's left for me when Brandon finally runs out of people to hurt? Will I be the next one to suffer his wrath? Or will I finally find the courage to stand up and say something before it's too late?

Time is running out. And I'm not sure how much longer I can just stand by and watch.

ENTRY #39
14 JUNE 2014

I've been watching Brandon's relationship with Katie for months now. At first, she seemed like a fresh breath of air—a confident girl, assertive, independent, full of life. She had this spark that made her stand out. She was one of the few who didn't seem to be intimidated by Brandon's usual bravado. But now, it's like watching someone unravel. She's not the same person she used to be.

It's eerie, really. Katie, the girl who would laugh loudly and talk about her dreams, is now hollowed out. She walks around like a shadow of herself, eyes glazed over, always looking at the ground. The few times I've caught her looking at Brandon, there's this desperate, pleading look in her eyes, like she's waiting for something—validation, a kindness, a spark of the man she fell in love with. But it never comes. I know she's trying to hold on, but it's like she's slipping, inch by inch. It's as if she's become addicted to something she can't name, but it's clear it's not just Brandon's attention. It's something darker—something deeper than what they have.

They're not like other couples. They're not a match made in heaven. They're like an old married couple who have been together for far too long—exhausted, worn out, and trapped in a toxic dependency. Katie's clinginess has become almost suffocating, like she needs Brandon's presence to breathe. Every time I see them together, she's glued to him, as if she's afraid to let him go, even for a second. It's like she can't live without him, but the sad truth is, she's dying because of him.

I can see it in her face. Her once bright, confident smile has faded into something hollow. Her skin has lost its glow, and her posture is slumped, as though she's carrying an invisible weight that's dragging her down. She's starting to look unhealthy, too. I've seen her hands shake when she holds a pen, her eyes bloodshot in the mornings, and she always seems tired—exhausted to the bone.

I wouldn't be surprised if she's on something. I can't put my finger on it, but there's something about the way she moves, the way she speaks—or doesn't speak—that feels off. Maybe it's the way her words stumble out, slow and disconnected. Maybe it's the way she avoids eye contact when she talks to people. There's no spark left in her, no fire. Just a cold emptiness. It makes me wonder if Brandon has done this to her—if he's managed to break her down until she's nothing more than a shell of the girl she used to be.

But then again, I can't help but wonder if she's complicit in it. Does she know what's happening to her? Does she want this? Or is she too far gone to even care? Either way, the person she is now feels like a stranger to me. The Katie I once knew is nowhere to be found.

What's even more unsettling is watching Brandon. It's like he's feeding off her misery. There's no tenderness in his eyes when he looks at her anymore. There's no care, no love. It's like he's numb to her suffering, watching it like an artist studying their creation. I've seen the way he treats her—sometimes cold, sometimes manipulative, but always in control. He's become this twisted version of himself, taking pleasure in her dependence on him. It's as if he sees her misery as a sign of power.

At first, I couldn't understand why someone like Katie, who seemed so strong, would get caught in his web. But now I get it. Brandon is good at what he does. He knows how to make you feel like you need him. He knows how to twist the truth and make you doubt yourself. He's always been good at that—always playing people, making them think they can't live without him. But now, it's like he's taken it to another level. He doesn't just control people anymore—he breaks them. He ruins them.

I overheard a conversation between some of the other girls in the class yesterday. They were talking about Katie, about how she's been looking worse lately. One of them mentioned that she's been skipping class, hiding out in the bathroom, and they said she looks like she's "on something." I don't know how much of that is true, but it doesn't surprise me. I've seen the signs too. She's too far gone to save herself, and Brandon has already claimed her. He's wrapped her up in his web, and now she's trapped in it.

I don't know why I'm writing this down. Maybe it's because I want to remember how this all started. How it started with a girl who was full of life and ended with a girl who barely exists anymore. Maybe I'm writing it down because I'm scared—scared of what might happen to Katie, scared of what might happen to Brandon next, and scared of what I might become if I continue to watch this from the sidelines.

I used to think that if I just stayed quiet, stayed out of the way, everything would be okay. But now, I'm not so sure. It's hard to stay quiet when you see someone slowly falling apart in front of your eyes. It's hard to keep your head down when you know that something terrible is happening, and you don't know how to stop it.

Brandon has found a way to control everything around him. He's found a way to break people and rebuild them in his own image. And I can't help but wonder—when will it stop? When will he go too far?

I want to say something to Katie. I want to reach out to her and tell her that she doesn't have to live like this. But I know she won't listen. I know she's too far gone, too wrapped up in Brandon's toxic grip to even see what's happening to her. And I know that if I try, Brandon will come for me too.

This is the kind of life Brandon has created. A life where everyone around him is either broken or complicit in the destruction. And I'm starting to realize that maybe the only way to escape this is to break free myself. Maybe the only way to survive is to walk away, to stop watching as everything falls apart.

But even then, I'm not sure if I'll ever truly escape it. Once you've seen what Brandon is capable of, once you've witnessed the destruction he's caused, there's no going back. You can't unsee it. You can't forget it.

And so, I'm left here, watching as he destroys everything and everyone around him. Watching as Katie fades further and further away, as Brandon grows darker and more dangerous. And I wonder—what will happen when there's no one left for him to hurt? What happens when he finally pushes everyone away? Will he stop, or will he keep going, pushing further into the abyss?

Only time will tell. But I fear that by the time it's over, it will be too late for any of us to save ourselves.

ENTRY #40
13 July 2015

It's strange. We're finally in our Senior years, and I've been noticing something unsettling about Brandon. For the past few weeks, he's been staring at me. Not in the way people sometimes do when they're lost in thought, but with something... more. It's hard to describe, but it feels like an intrusion, like he's looking through me instead of at me. There's this coldness in his gaze, and it makes me uncomfortable every time our eyes meet.

I don't know if he's aware of how intense it is, or if he's deliberately trying to make me feel uneasy. Maybe it's all in my head, but I don't think so. This isn't like the casual glances from before, the ones you'd expect between old friends. This is something else. Something predatory, almost.

I've tried to shake it off, but it's hard not to notice. Every time I look over at him, I catch him watching. He doesn't seem to care that I see him, either. The moments are fleeting, but when they happen, they hang in the air, making my skin crawl. It's like he knows something that I don't, and he's waiting for me to figure it out. But I don't want to know.

I don't want to be around him. I don't want to look at him. I keep telling myself it's just me being paranoid, but I can't shake the feeling that he's changed. He's always been a manipulator, but now it's like he's evolved into something darker. Something that isn't satisfied with just controlling others—he wants something more, something that I'm terrified to even think about.

He's still surrounded by his usual group of cronies—guys who hang on his every word, who laugh at his jokes, who follow his lead. But even they seem to be a little more distant, a little more wary. Even they seem to be realizing, on some level, that there's something wrong with Brandon.

I wonder if they notice what I've been seeing, or if they're just as blind to it as I used to be. I wonder if Brandon has been isolating himself, pushing people away, so that he can focus on whatever dark obsession he's developed. He's always been good at manipulating people, but now it feels like he's trying to manipulate something bigger, something scarier. I don't know if it's me or someone else, but I don't think I'm the only one who's been targeted.

And I'm scared. I'm scared of what's coming, of what's already started. I don't know how to get out of this, how to escape whatever hold he has on me, on all of us. It's like he's always two steps ahead, planning something I can't even begin to understand.

ENTRY #41
14 JULY 2015

It happened again today.

Brandon stared at me with that familiar intensity, a look that no longer felt casual or benign. His eyes were fixed on me from across the room, his expression unreadable. It wasn't new; this had been going on for weeks now, but today it was different. Today, it felt like he was waiting for me to notice. And I couldn't avoid it anymore.

I could feel my heart pounding in my chest as I tried to focus on the lesson. But it wasn't working. The words on the board blurred, my mind circling around what I knew was coming. I needed to confront him, to understand what was going on inside his head.

So I did.

After the bell rang, I stayed in my seat for a moment, pretending to pack my things. But I didn't need to pretend anymore. I stood up and walked straight toward Brandon. He looked up, the corner of his mouth twitching into a smirk that didn't reach his eyes.

"Hey," I said, trying to sound casual, though my voice cracked slightly. "What's with the staring?"

Brandon didn't respond immediately. His gaze flickered over me, a moment of calculation, before he stood up, slowly, his tall frame looming over me. "You're observant," he muttered, the words edged with something I couldn't place. "You've been watching me for a while, haven't you?"

I swallowed hard, the words catching in my throat. "I asked you first."

He leaned in slightly, his breath warm against my skin. "Fine. You want to know? Follow me."

I didn't hesitate. There was something dark about the way he said it, something that told me I couldn't just let this slide.

I followed him out of the classroom, down the narrow hallways, until we reached the back door. Outside, the sun was low in the sky, casting long shadows over the campus. Brandon led me toward the far corner of the school, a secluded area where the trees and tall fences obscured us from view. We were alone now, the quietness pressing down on me.

Brandon stopped and turned to face me, his expression now serious, even somber. There was a distance in his eyes, a cloudiness that made me uneasy.

"What do you think of me?" he asked, the question hanging between us like a challenge.

I hesitated, taken aback by the suddenness of it. I had never really thought about it that way. He wasn't just the same guy I used to know anymore—he had changed. He had become something else, something harder, colder.

"I think you've changed," I said, voice steady despite my nerves. "I think you've become... unpredictable."

He scoffed, running a hand through his hair. "Unpredictable, huh? You're too kind. But that's what you always thought of me, wasn't it? That I was a mess of contradictions. Well, you're not wrong."

I didn't know how to respond to that, so I said nothing, letting the silence stretch.

Brandon exhaled sharply, almost as if he had been holding something in for a long time. He turned his gaze toward the ground, his posture suddenly deflated. "You want to know why I stare at you? Why I've been so... fixated?" he asked, his voice low.

I nodded, unable to keep my curiosity at bay.

"It's because I can't stop seeing you," he said, his voice distant. "I can't stop seeing what you've become."

I blinked, confused. "What do you mean?"

He paused, then finally looked up at me, his eyes full of something dangerous. "You're so fucking normal. You act like everything is okay. Like you've got it all figured out. But I know what's going on behind those perfect little eyes of yours. I see how you look at me."

My pulse quickened, but I kept my expression neutral, even as his words sunk in. "I don't look at you like anything."

Brandon's lips curled into a sardonic smile. "Of course you do. You've always looked at me like that. Like I'm a freak. Like I'm broken."

There was so much venom in his voice that it made my skin crawl. For a moment, I didn't know what to say, but I couldn't back down now.

"You're not a freak," I finally muttered, "but you're not the person I used to know either."

Brandon's smirk faltered, and for a fleeting second, I saw a glimmer of something vulnerable in his eyes. Then, just as quickly, it disappeared, replaced by a cold hardness.

"You don't know anything about me," he said, the words sharp and final.

A long silence followed. The tension between us thickened, palpable, suffocating. And then, without warning, he spoke again.

"Do you want to know what happened to me? What really fucked me up?" he asked, voice barely above a whisper.

I nodded slowly, feeling the weight of the moment settle around us.

Brandon took a step back, leaning against the wall, his expression unreadable. "It's not just me. It's my family. You don't know what I've had to deal with... what I've seen."

I was silent, waiting for him to continue. This was the moment, I realized. The moment where the mask would fall.

He let out a shaky breath, his hand shaking slightly as he ran it through his hair again. "My dad... he used to do things. Things you wouldn't believe. I was five when I first saw it. Him with some woman. I didn't even know her name. He'd beat them... and fuck them. Right in front of me. He made me watch."

His voice was tight now, the words coming out strained, like he was forcing them through a clenched throat. "It was sick. And I couldn't do anything. I was just a kid."

I stood frozen, a part of me wanting to leave, wanting to run from this nightmare, but another part of me was drawn in, unable to look away.

Brandon's eyes flickered briefly with something resembling pain before he continued, his voice becoming colder, more detached. "My sister... she became a prostitute. To feed us. To survive. And when my dad found out... He didn't care. He took her, right in front of me. He fucking raped her. My own sister. And I couldn't do a thing. I was just a kid. But I... I had to call the cops. I had to do something."

The air around us seemed to constrict as he spoke, his words wrapping around me, suffocating me with the weight of his past. He wasn't just broken; he was shattered.

"And that was it," he finished, his voice almost hollow. "That was the moment I realized that the world doesn't care. People are fucking monsters, and if you don't fight back, they'll eat you alive."

I didn't know what to say. His story—his reality—was something so far beyond what I could comprehend that I felt like I was suffocating. But somehow, I knew that this wasn't the end. It was just the beginning.

The silence that followed Brandon's words felt like it stretched for miles. My heartbeat hammered in my chest, my breath shallow as I processed what he had just shared. He had said these things so matter-of-factly, as if they were memories rather than traumatic experiences. He looked at me, his eyes searching, and I saw it then: the damage was deeper than I'd ever imagined.

I didn't know what to say. The weight of his confession sat between us like a mountain, and I didn't have the tools to scale it. He had just told me about his father's brutality, his sister's desperate survival, and the unimaginable cruelty they had both endured. It was so much more than I had ever imagined, and I couldn't even begin to understand what that kind of history would do to a person.

Brandon shifted his weight, his hands clenched into fists at his sides. He looked away, staring out into the school grounds.

I wanted to say something, to offer him comfort, but the words felt hollow. What could I say to something like this?

Finally, after what felt like an eternity, Brandon spoke again, his voice quieter but no less intense. "You want to know what it did to me?" he asked, his eyes now distant, as if he was seeing something far beyond the school campus. "It made me hate people. I hate them, I really do. They're all fucking liars. They'll lie to your face and pretend like everything is okay, but underneath it all, they're all the same. They're just as fucked up as my dad. They'll hurt you, and they'll make you watch, and no one will care."

His words cut through the air, jagged and raw, leaving me feeling like I'd just been struck.

"I get it," he continued, his voice growing colder, harder. "People like me, people like you—we're all just playing pretend. We pretend like we're normal, like we're good. But deep down, we're all just like my dad. We're all just waiting for the right moment to snap."

I felt my stomach tighten. I didn't know what to say. I wanted to tell him that not everyone was like that, that there was still good in the world, but I couldn't get the words to come out. Instead, I just stood there, waiting for him to keep going.

Brandon didn't seem to notice my discomfort. His gaze was still distant, as if he was speaking more to himself than to me. "You don't know what it's like," he said, almost bitterly. "You don't know what it's like to see your own sister get fucked over and over again by your father. You don't know what it's like to watch the people you love fall apart and not be able to do a damn thing about it."

The anger in his voice grew, and I realized that this was something much darker than just a personal vendetta—it was the culmination of years of trauma. He had been carrying all of this inside him for so long, and now, it was spilling out, uncontrollable.

"I used to think I was different," Brandon said, his voice lowering as he stared at the ground. "I thought if I could just get out of that house, get away from him, I'd be okay. But the truth is, you don't escape something like that. It gets inside you. It eats you up. You can't just leave it behind."

There was a long silence as he seemed to withdraw into himself. I didn't know what to do, what to say. I was trying to make sense of what he had just told me, but it was like trying to understand a language I didn't speak.

"And then there's my sister," Brandon continued, his voice tinged with disgust. "She did what she had to do. I can't blame her for that. She was just trying to survive, to give me a chance to make it out of there. But I hate her for it. I hate her for what she became. I hate that she became just like him—used and broken."

I felt a wave of guilt wash over me. He was right—his sister had been doing what she thought was necessary. But now, hearing him speak about it like this, I could see the impact it had on him, the way it had twisted everything inside of him.

"I called the cops that night," Brandon said quietly, almost as if speaking to himself. "I called them on my own father. But it didn't matter. He still got away with everything. He didn't even get jail time. They gave him a slap on the wrist, and he went right back to doing what he was doing."

The bitterness in his voice was palpable. I could see the years of anger and resentment that had built up inside of him. He had tried to do the right thing, but the world had failed him.

"I'm not like you, man," he said, his eyes locking onto mine with a cold, intense gaze. "I'm not just some kid trying to find his way. I don't have a future. I don't have anything. I've been ruined for too long."

The finality in his words hit me like a punch to the gut. Brandon had been broken so thoroughly that he had no hope left. There was nothing I could say to fix it, no way to undo the damage that had been done.

I didn't know how to comfort him, but I knew that I couldn't just walk away. Not after hearing everything he'd just shared with me.

"You're not ruined," I said quietly. "You don't have to be like your dad."

Brandon looked at me, his eyes dark and unreadable. "You don't get it. It's too late for me."

I wanted to argue, to tell him that there was always a chance to change, but I knew it wouldn't matter. He had already made up his mind.

For a moment, we just stood there, in the quiet of the secluded corner, the weight of everything hanging in the air between us. Finally, Brandon spoke again, his voice softer now, almost resigned.

"I've been trying to figure out how to get out of this mess," he said, "but I don't know how. I don't know if I can. I don't know if I want to."

And that was when I realized: this was no longer just about Brandon. This wasn't some troubled teenager going through a phase. This was a person who had been broken by forces far beyond his control, someone who was sinking deeper into a darkness that I didn't think he would ever crawl out of.

I didn't say anything else after that. I just nodded, and Brandon turned away, walking off into the distance, leaving me standing there, alone with my thoughts.

ENTRY #42
16 July 2015

After everything that had happened, I felt this strange, desperate need to reach out. Maybe it was out of empathy, or maybe I just needed to believe there was still something human left in Brandon. I invited him over to my place after school to play video games. It was a stupid, simple offer, but for some reason, I thought it might help.

To my surprise, he agreed. I half expected him to make some excuse, but he didn't.

We sat there for an hour or two, lost in the game, the tension easing as we laughed at each other's mistakes and joked about the stupid things we did in the game. For a brief moment, it felt like we were just two kids hanging out again, like nothing had changed.

But then, without warning, Brandon stopped playing. His hands, which had been clutching the controller, dropped to his sides. I turned to look at him, and his face had gone pale. His eyes were wide, but they weren't focused. They were unfocused, lost in some distant thought.

Then, something I hadn't expected happened: he broke down in front of me.

The tears came first, slow and steady, rolling down his cheeks. His voice cracked as he spoke, like he was trying to force words past a tight knot in his throat. "I'm sorry," he whispered, barely audible. "I'm sorry for everything I've done to you. For everything... everything I've done to everyone."

I sat there frozen, unsure of how to react. The Brandon I knew didn't apologize. He never admitted weakness. It was always about power, control, dominance. But here he was, broken. For a moment, I thought I might've imagined it, but then I saw the raw, tortured expression in his eyes, and I realized: this was real. He was letting me see the damage for the first time.

"I've been so fucking lost," he continued, voice shaking now. "You were always there, and I... I ruined it. I ruined everything. You're the only one who was ever there for me. You were my one true friend, and I fucked that up."

The words hit me harder than I expected. I didn't know what to say, so I just sat there, still unsure how to process everything he was pouring out. It was like I'd been handed a puzzle, pieces I couldn't quite fit together, but I knew that whatever it was—whatever he was confessing—it had been a long time coming.

"I don't know how to fix it," he said, his voice barely above a whisper. "I don't know how to fix me."

For the first time in years, I saw the person Brandon used to be—the vulnerable kid who was scared and alone. I couldn't reconcile that with the person he had become. But for a moment, just a fleeting moment, I felt something stir within me—something like hope, or maybe just pity. I wanted to believe he could change, that somehow, we could get back to what we had.

But deep down, I knew better. This wasn't going to be a simple fix. And yet, I couldn't help but feel that the mask he'd been wearing had cracked, just enough for me to glimpse the real Brandon beneath. It wasn't enough to save him, but it was enough to leave me questioning everything I thought I knew about him.

"Don't apologize," I finally managed to say, my voice quiet. "We're not there yet. You've done a lot of damage, Brandon. But I'm not sure you can fix everything. Not in one night."

He nodded, wiping his face with the sleeve of his shirt, trying to regain some composure. But I could see it in his eyes—the guilt, the shame. It was all there, clear as day.

"I don't expect you to forgive me," he said quietly, his voice raw. "I don't even know if I deserve it. But I needed you to know. I needed to say it."

And then, as quickly as the moment had started, it ended. He stood up, wiping his eyes one last time, his mask slipping back into place. "Thanks for listening," he muttered, not meeting my eyes. "But I've gotta go."

After the passionate embrace, the room was silent except for the soft hum of the old video game console in the corner. Brandon's breath was ragged, his eyes dark and searching as they locked onto mine. I could see the conflict swirling beneath his skin, a storm of emotion and disbelief, fear and sadness. We stayed there for a moment, just holding each other, until the golden light of the setting sun started to fade, casting long shadows around us. Brandon looked down, his expression unreadable, and I could feel the weight of everything we had just shared pressing down on both of us.

ENTRY #43
17 JULY 2015

I woke up today with an unusual sense of calm, as though the clouds had parted and there was a faint glimmer of sunshine. My thoughts were still clouded by what happened between Brandon and me, but there was a certain sense of peace in it. It felt like a moment of clarity, something between us had shifted.

I went through my morning routine, and even in the halls of school, I could sense a subtle shift in the way the other students behaved. It wasn't until I walked into the homeroom that I saw it—police officers. They were standing by the door, speaking with Ms. Thompson, our homeroom teacher, in hushed tones. The look on her face—she was almost... blank. Disconnected. The atmosphere in the room instantly thickened.

The whispers came next—disjointed, anxious. I could hear bits of it as I sat down at my desk, trying to ignore the tension in the air. The name that kept repeating itself among the hushed voices was Brandon's.

"Did you hear? He was arrested... Euphoria... drugs... He's been dealing..."

At first, I couldn't make sense of it. Euphoria? The rumors about the new drug had been circulating for weeks now, but hearing it attached to Brandon was different. This was no longer just idle gossip—this was reality, as if the world had shifted in some irreversible way. The shock was heavy in my chest. I couldn't quite grasp it. Brandon, the guy who had always been in control, the guy who commanded attention without even trying—arrested. The thought felt almost absurd, like a joke too cruel to be real.

Ms. Thompson finally addressed the class. She was calm, unnervingly so, as she explained that the police were there to take care of some... "unresolved matters." I could tell she was holding back more than she was letting on, but the tension was palpable. We were dismissed early that day, and as the bell rang, I stood frozen in place, not knowing what to do or where to go.

I wanted to see Brandon. I needed to. I didn't know why—I just felt this strange compulsion to be near him. He'd been such a constant presence, and now, without him, everything felt off-balance. He was always the one who controlled the room, the one who got what he wanted. And now? Now he was being dragged into the system, just like everyone else who had ever been caught in the web he'd woven around himself.

I couldn't escape the feeling that something had broken. A small part of me felt guilty, like I'd played a role in all of this, like if I had spoken up sooner, if I had just stopped pretending, maybe this wouldn't have happened.

I walked to my locker after class, my mind a whirl of thoughts, but I was distracted by the sounds of hurried footsteps behind me. I turned, and it was him—Bradley, one of Brandon's old friends. His face was tight with fear, and there was a wild look in his eyes. His voice cracked as he spoke.

"They've got him, man. They're taking him in. His dad... I heard his dad's been mixed up in this stuff for years, but Brandon? I never thought..."

Bradley's words were a blur, but the essence of it stuck with me. Brandon had been dealing drugs—Euphoria, yes—but it wasn't just the drugs. It was everything that had built up around him—the years of manipulation, the power games, the twisted sense of control. The way he had always seemed untouchable. I had been so drawn into him, into his world, that I never stopped to think about how deep it went.

I felt a weight settle in my chest. Brandon had been more than just a friend—he had been a figure in my life. A constant, an anchor in a world that had otherwise felt chaotic. I had tried to understand him, tried to find the reason behind his actions, but now it was clear. Brandon wasn't just a victim of circumstance. He was a product of his own choices.

And in some way, I was too. I had allowed him to pull me in, to make me complicit in his twisted games. It wasn't just the drugs. It was the manipulation, the lies, the way he twisted everyone around him into doing his bidding.

I stayed at school for a while after the incident, walking the halls like a ghost, trying to make sense of everything. The other students were no different—whispers, furtive glances, everyone trying to make sense of something that didn't make sense.

I wanted to see Brandon. I wanted to understand what had happened, what had led him to this moment. But I couldn't. Not yet. Maybe not ever.

As the day ended and the campus began to empty, I found myself standing alone at the gates of the school, staring out at the street where the police cars had pulled up only hours before. The finality of it all hit me hard.

Brandon's arrest was just another chapter in a story that had been unfolding for years. A story of a boy who had never been able to escape his past, of a boy who had always used power to hide his weakness.

I didn't know if I could ever fix things. Maybe I wasn't supposed to. But I couldn't shake the feeling that this was just the beginning of something far worse. Something darker. And all I could do was wait and watch as the story unfolded around me.

What would become of Brandon? Would he face the consequences of his actions? Or would he slip further into the darkness, dragging everyone around him with him?

All I knew was that whatever happened next, nothing would ever be the same.

Entry #44
Present Day, Interrogation Room

Brandon leans back in his chair, the metallic creak of it loud in the otherwise quiet room. His hands are folded in front of him, fingers tapping rhythmically against the table. It's a strange sensation, sitting here again, after all this time. In this sterile room, in this charged atmosphere, he's no longer the boy I used to know. But then again, I'm not the same either. None of us are.

Brandon's voice breaks the silence. "You want to know how I got here? How I became... this?" He doesn't wait for me to answer. It's like he already knows. He has always known. "You've been asking that for years. I can see it in your eyes, how you keep looking at me like you want some kind of explanation for what happened. Like if you just understood, you'd be able to forgive me." He pauses, looking directly at me, as though daring me to deny it.

I don't say anything. His words sting more than I thought they would, but I keep my mouth shut. I want to hear it, all of it. The pieces of the puzzle that I've never understood. The timeline of events that led to this moment.

Brandon exhales slowly, almost like a sigh of resignation, and begins to speak again, his voice quieter now, as if he's preparing to unravel something that has haunted him for years.

"It started with my dad. You remember him, right? How he was always drunk and out of it. How he'd come home smelling like beer and cigarettes, stumbling around and yelling at us. But that's not the worst part." Brandon's eyes flicker to the side, and for a split second, I catch a glimpse of something raw, something vulnerable. Then it's gone.

"He wasn't just a drunk. He was a monster," Brandon continues, his words growing more charged with each syllable. "He used to... God, this is hard to talk about. He used to hit my mom. Beat her until she couldn't move. I had to watch it. I couldn't do anything. I was just a kid. And when he was done with her, he'd turn to me. Sometimes he'd make me watch, sometimes... sometimes he'd make me join in. He didn't care. He didn't care what I wanted. He didn't care that I was a kid. He just wanted someone to hurt."

Brandon's words cut into the silence, and for a moment, I don't know what to say. I don't know if there's anything to say. What do you say to someone who's been through hell and is finally letting you in?

"The worst part? The part that fucked me up the most?" Brandon leans forward now, his eyes locking onto mine. "It's that I knew it was wrong. But I didn't know how to stop it. I thought that was just how the world worked, that the people you loved were supposed to hurt you. That pain was normal. It was part of growing up." He shakes his head, as though trying to shake off the memory. "But it wasn't normal. Not at all."

I nod, understanding a little more now. But there's so much more to this story. I can feel it hanging in the air, thick with unspoken words.

Brandon presses on. "When my mom couldn't take it anymore, she left. She just up and left one night. She didn't even say goodbye. She didn't even try to fight for us. It was like she gave up on me. She gave up on us. And when she left, everything just fell apart."

I can't help but feel a sense of pity for him, though I know I shouldn't. It's the same pity that I felt when I saw him standing alone in the playground as a child, but now it feels heavier, more complicated. I hate myself for still feeling it.

"I don't know how to explain it, but after she left, I just... I lost it. I got worse. I started doing things. Things I can't take back. I made a mess of everything. I started to hang out with the wrong crowd. The guys who didn't care about anything but getting high and doing whatever they wanted. That's when I started to drink. To smoke. And yeah, it felt good at first. But it didn't make the pain go away. It just numbed it for a little while."

Brandon pauses, and for a moment, I can almost see the boy I used to know—the one who still had hope, even if it was buried beneath the surface. But then he continues, and I realize that kid is long gone.

"It wasn't just the drugs, though. It was the girls. I started to see them as objects. Like, it wasn't about who they were, it was about what I could take from them. I don't know when it happened exactly, but one day I realized I was just using them. For sex. For control. For something to fill the emptiness. And when I couldn't get what I wanted, when they fought back or wouldn't give me what I thought I deserved, that's when things got dark. I got angry. I started to hurt them."

I feel a chill run through me as Brandon's words settle in my mind. I knew he was bad, but I never realized how deep it went. I never thought he would be capable of this.

"The thing is," he says, almost as if he's talking to himself now, "I never thought it would go that far. I never thought I'd get into the whole... rape thing. But the more I did it, the easier it got. It was like this switch flipped inside me. I didn't care anymore. I didn't care about anyone but myself. I didn't care about you. I didn't care about Pearl. I didn't care about anyone. I just wanted to take what I wanted, whenever I wanted."

Brandon's face hardens, and I can see the weight of his words on him. He looks like he's been carrying something for a long time, and now that he's finally letting it out, it's breaking him.

"I didn't even realize what I was becoming. Not until it was too late," he says, his voice almost a whisper now. "The more I did, the more I wanted. And when I started selling the drugs, the Euphoria, I felt unstoppable. Like nothing could touch me. I had money, power, control. And when people got in my way, I took care of them. I did what I had to do to stay on top."

There's a pause. Brandon leans back in his chair again, his face a mask of exhaustion. "But that's when everything started to spiral out of control. I did things. Terrible things. Things I wish I could take back. But I can't. And now... now I'm paying for it."

His eyes meet mine, and for the first time since we started this conversation, I see something like regret in them. It's brief, but it's there. "The drugs, the violence, the girls—none of it mattered in the end. It didn't fix anything. It just made it worse. And now... now I've gone too far."

He looks down at his hands, his fingers trembling slightly as if the weight of his actions is finally catching up to him. "I'm not proud of what I've done. But I'm not sorry either. Not anymore. Because I did what I had to do to survive."

The room is silent for a moment, and I can't help but wonder if I've been talking to a monster all along. Or if this is just the broken shell of a person who was destroyed by the world around him. I don't know. But I do know that this, all of it, has been building for years. And now, it's too late for any of us to fix it.

Brandon's voice breaks the silence once more. "I don't want your pity. I don't want your sympathy. I just want you to understand. Understand what I had to become to survive. Understand why I did what I did."

The room is thick with silence as I let Brandon's words hang in the air, the weight of everything he's said pressing down on us both. I had been listening intently, trying to follow the path he had taken, to understand the twisted steps that led him to this moment. I'm not sure I'm any closer to understanding, but I'm willing to keep listening.

Finally, I ask the question that's been gnawing at me for hours, maybe even years.

"How do you feel about me, Brandon?"

The words leave my mouth before I can stop them, and for a moment, I regret asking. It's too late, though. The question has already been posed, and I can't take it back.

Brandon doesn't answer immediately. Instead, he tilts his head, his eyes narrowing as if the question has caught him off guard. I watch his expression shift from one of stoic detachment to something else—something closer to confusion, maybe even vulnerability.

After what feels like an eternity, he speaks, his voice low and hesitant. "What do you mean?"

I swallow hard, suddenly realizing the gravity of what I've asked. "I mean, after everything that's happened, after everything I've seen... how do you feel about me? About what we had, or what we didn't have?" I let the words linger in the air, unsure of where they'll land.

Brandon's lips press together in a thin line as he considers my question. His eyes shift, flickering around the room as if he's searching for something—some answer that will make sense of everything. But there's no easy answer. There never has been with Brandon.

"You're asking me how I feel about you now?" He finally asks, his voice a little rougher than before. I nod, not sure what else to do. "I don't know. I don't think I ever knew, honestly. We were... friends, I guess. But I don't know if I ever really knew how to be a friend." He lets out a bitter laugh, his eyes momentarily closing as if he's lost in some distant memory.

"You were the only one who didn't just take from me," he continues, his tone softer now. "You actually saw me. Not just... the mess I was, but the parts of me I tried to hide. Maybe that's why I pushed you away so much. Because you saw things I didn't want anyone to see. And it scared the hell out of me."

I sit still, processing his words. It's strange to hear him admit it, to hear him acknowledge something I've suspected for so long but never dared to put into words. It doesn't make sense, though. How could he have seen me as someone who understood him when he treated me like his enemy for so long?

Brandon looks at me again, his gaze sharp. "But I don't know if I can say I care about you, not in the way you want me to. I can't care about anyone. Not after everything. Not after what I've done. I tried, you know? I tried to make something out of what we had, but it was always just a fucking game to me." He scoffs, shaking his head. "I guess I used you, just like I used everyone else."

The confession hits me like a slap in the face. I want to be angry, but the words are stuck in my throat. Part of me wants to scream at him, to demand an apology for all the years of manipulation and pain. But another part of me—the part that has always felt sorry for him, even when I shouldn't—just listens. And I realize that it's not the anger I feel right now. It's... loss.

Brandon exhales slowly, his shoulders sagging. "I don't know what I'm supposed to feel. You're asking me to care about you, and I don't even know how to care about myself. It's like, everything I've ever done, everything I've ever been... it's all been about trying to fill this hole inside of me. And maybe, just maybe, you were the only one who didn't try to use me to fill it. But I don't know how to... give back. I don't know how to make it right."

The words are painful to hear, but they're the truth. And for some reason, I can't bring myself to resent him for saying them. I can't bring myself to hate him, even though I know I should.

"Brandon," I say, my voice quieter than usual, "what does it take to fix all of this? What do you think you need to make it right? Can you fix it?"

Brandon looks at me, and for a moment, I swear I see the faintest flicker of regret in his eyes. It's fleeting, almost imperceptible, but it's there. He doesn't say anything for a long time, his gaze distant as if he's trying to sort through the mess of his own emotions.

"I don't think there's anything that can fix it now," he finally says, his voice barely above a whisper. "Maybe once, I thought I could be better. But now... now I'm too far gone. And so are you. I don't know what you expect from me. You want some kind of closure, but I don't think it works like that. You can't fix people like me. You can't fix people who've already broken beyond repair."

I don't know how to respond to that. I want to argue, to tell him that it's not too late, that people can change, but the words feel hollow. He's right. I've spent too many years trying to piece together the fragments of our broken friendship, trying to make sense of the destruction he's caused in my life.

I'm not sure what I expected from this conversation. Maybe I thought that hearing his side would give me some kind of peace, or that I would understand why things turned out the way they did. But now, after hearing it all, I'm left with more questions than answers.

Brandon's eyes meet mine again, and for a brief moment, we just stare at each other. There's nothing left to say, not really. The silence between us feels heavy, like the weight of all the years we've wasted, all the chances we missed.

Finally, Brandon stands up, his chair scraping loudly against the floor. "I guess that's all there is to it. I've told you what you wanted to hear. I don't know what you'll do with it, but that's the truth. Take it or leave it."

Before I can respond, he walks toward the door, his footsteps echoing in the quiet room. He pauses just before exiting, turning back to face me. His expression is unreadable, distant.

"I don't know what happens next," he says, his voice softer now. "But whatever it is... it's not going to be good. For either of us."

And with that, he leaves. The door clicks shut behind him, leaving me alone in the interrogation room once again.

I sit there for a long time, processing everything he's said. It feels like the end of something—maybe the end of a chapter, or maybe the end of the entire story. I don't know. But one thing is certain: I'm not sure I'll ever be able to look at Brandon the same way again.

Criminology Case Study: Brandon Harris

C ompiled by: ?, Criminologist
Date of Report: July 18, 2023

Early Life and Development

Brandon Harris's early years were marred by trauma and neglect. Raised in a volatile environment, his father's abuse set the stage for a deeply troubled childhood. Brandon's earliest memories were shaped by violence, emotional neglect, and exposure to criminal behavior. His father, a known drug dealer, often engaged in degrading acts of violence, including the assault of women in front of Brandon and his sister. The subsequent trauma, especially the sexual abuse of his sister, became the foundation for Brandon's emotional and psychological scars.

Brandon's early years were devoid of protective or nurturing figures, making his coping mechanisms maladaptive and leading to a disjointed emotional development. His experiences with violence and degradation skewed his sense of self-worth, fostering a profound lack of empathy and a deep sense of anger toward the world.

Teenage Years and Early Warning Signs

As Brandon entered his adolescent years, his behavior began to reflect the growing internal chaos. His relationships with others were strained, and he developed a pattern of manipulation, aggression, and an unhealthy need for dominance, particularly over female peers. Brandon's emotional volatility manifested as promiscuity and increasingly reckless behavior. He began using his charm and physicality to exert control over others, particularly in the realm of sexual manipulation. His relationships with girls, in particular, often involved coercion, creating an atmosphere of fear and dependency.

Despite the outward bravado, Brandon struggled with a pervasive sense of powerlessness, especially regarding his abusive home life. However, instead of seeking help or healing, he sought refuge in power and control over others. His erratic behavior, which included violence toward peers and a growing addiction to drugs, further isolated him from the few who might have otherwise been positive influences.

Brandon's behavior became notably darker during high school, where rumors began circulating about his involvement in sexual assaults and other violent incidents. His proclivity for control extended into every aspect of his life, including how he interacted with friends and classmates. This manifested in a terrifying ability to manipulate and use people for his own ends.

The Escalation of Violence and Criminal Behavior

B randon's descent into criminality reached a peak during his high school years. By then, he had fully embraced his identity as a violent, manipulative individual. He surrounded himself with like-minded peers, using his charm to seduce, control, and exploit others. His involvement in drug use and distribution, particularly with a drug known as Euphoria, placed him on a direct path toward legal trouble.

It wasn't until Brandon was arrested for drug-related charges that his behavior began to draw serious attention from authorities. He was sent to prison, a formative experience that would shape his personality further. Prison, where he was exposed to even more extreme violence, further solidified his anger and sense of powerlessness. The abuse he suffered in prison nurtured an even darker side of him, one that was motivated by an overwhelming need for revenge against the world that had mistreated him.

Post-Prison Behavior and Continuing Crimes

U pon his release from prison, Brandon's actions grew even more violent and vengeful. With an intense desire to prove himself, he turned to increasingly extreme methods of exerting control over others. He engaged in a series of heinous crimes, each more grotesque than the last, driven by an unchecked rage. His connections with old friends and criminals from his past remained, allowing him to continue his illicit activities without much opposition.

Brandon's actions revealed a clear pattern: his crimes were a manifestation of his deep-seated anger and trauma. Each violent act, each exploitative relationship, seemed to serve as both a means of asserting dominance and a form of retaliation against the world that had wronged him. His lack of remorse was evident, as he never acknowledged the pain he caused others but instead justified his actions as a necessary course of action.

Psychological Analysis

Brandon exhibits signs of both Antisocial Personality Disorder (APD) and Narcissistic Personality Disorder (NPD). His lack of empathy, disregard for the rights of others, and manipulative behavior are hallmarks of APD, while his inflated sense of self-importance and need for control fit the criteria for NPD. These disorders, combined with the trauma he experienced during his formative years, have created a deeply disturbed individual with little to no regard for social norms or morality.

Brandon's behavior suggests a profound inability to connect with others in any meaningful way. His relationships are exploitative, and he uses others as tools to fulfill his desires. At the core of his psyche is a fractured individual who seeks to regain control over a world that he perceives as unfair. This desperation manifests in violence and manipulation, making him a dangerous individual.

Conclusion and Future Outlook

Brandon Harris is a prime example of how early trauma, neglect, and a toxic environment can create the perfect storm for the development of violent and manipulative behavior. From a young age, Brandon was exposed to unimaginable horrors, and instead of receiving help, he was left to internalize and act out his trauma. His criminal behavior escalated from childhood misdeeds to violent and deadly crimes, with little to no remorse for the suffering he caused others.

Brandon's time in prison further hardened him, deepening his feelings of anger and vengeance. His crimes, both before and after his incarceration, serve as a tragic illustration of how unresolved trauma can manifest in destructive ways. While his actions can be understood in the context of his past, they are not excusable, and his future remains uncertain. Without intervention, it is likely that his violent tendencies will continue to escalate, posing a significant risk to both himself and others.

Recommendations for Further Evaluation:

• Psychological assessment to further explore Brandon's underlying personality disorders, including potential treatments such as Cognitive Behavioral Therapy (CBT) to address his anger and aggression.

• Continued monitoring of Brandon's behavior to assess his risk for reoffending, particularly regarding violent crimes.

• Exploration of rehabilitation options, though the prognosis for individuals with his background remains uncertain.

E *nd of Report*

Did you love *The Signs Were There*? Then you should read *Tales of Millinggarde; Aether's Veil*[1] by NM Aster!

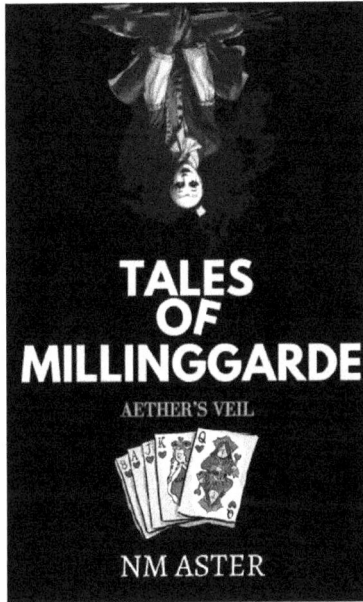

In a world where magic and science vie for dominance, Aether, a powerful nation fueled by mana, teeters on the edge of collapse as it depletes its own magical resources. Driven by desperation and ambition, Aether invades the technologically advanced but resource-rich nation of Millinggarde, a society that abandoned magic for scientific progress long ago. The brutal annexation of Millinggarde fractures its citizens, who are forced into submission or conscripted as cogs in Aether's relentless war machine. Despite this, a spirit of resistance stirs

1. https://books2read.com/u/bzy0n2

2. https://books2read.com/u/bzy0n2

within Millinggarde's oppressed populace, manifesting in daring acts of rebellion and the rise of enigmatic figures who challenge Aether's supremacy.

Amid the chaos, a masked vigilante known only as "The Pierrot" emerges, creating havoc that threatens to ignite a full-blown revolution. His acts of defiance sow discord not only in Millinggarde but within Aether's own ranks, forcing a cast of morally complex leaders to reconsider their loyalties and strategies. As the Pierrot's true intentions unfold, tensions between magic and technology reach a critical breaking point, setting the stage for an inevitable clash that could reshape both nations' destinies and expose long-buried secrets about the nature of power itself.

About the Author

NM Aster is an emerging author known for exploring complex, dark themes through deeply introspective narratives. Their works often delve into the human psyche, questioning the boundaries of morality, trauma, and identity. Aster's writing blends psychological insight with gritty realism, capturing the inner turmoil of characters on the brink of destruction. With a keen eye for detail and an unsettling sense of atmosphere, NM Aster crafts stories that are both thought-provoking and haunting, offering readers an exploration into the depths of human darkness and vulnerability.

9 798230 827054